John Hamilton Moore

The Practical Observer

John Hamilton Moore

The Practical Observer

ISBN/EAN: 9783741127564

Manufactured in Europe, USA, Canada, Australia, Japa

Cover: Foto ©Andreas Hilbeck / pixelio.de

Manufactured and distributed by brebook publishing software
(www.brebook.com)

John Hamilton Moore

The Practical Observer

THE

Practical Obſerver;

OR,

The NEW METHOD of FINDING

The LATITUDE at SEA,

By taking two ALTITUDES, either in the FORENOON or AFTERNOON.

And alſo, The NEW METHOD of FINDING

The LONGITUDE at SEA,

By taking the DISTANCE of the MOON from the SUN, or a FIXED STAR, &c.

Rendered EASY to the MEANEST CAPACITY.

By J. HAMILTON MOORE,

Author of the Practical Navigator, and Seaman's New Daily Aſſiſtant.

TO WHICH IS ADDED,

The New Solar Tables, and Table of Natural Sines,

With the Uſe of the Quadrant and Sextant.

LONDON, PRINTED:

And ſold by Mr. KNOX, in the Strand; by Meſſ. RICHARDSON and URQUHART, under the Royal-Exchange; and Mr. RIPLEY, at the Hermitage-Bridge, below the Tower.

M.DCC.LXXV.

TO THE

Right Honourable the Commiſſioners of Longitude, *the* Directors *of the Honourable* Eaſt India Company, *the* Admirals, *and other* Commanders *of his* MAJESTY's Royal Navy.

My LORDS and GENTLEMEN,

AS every attempt to elucidate matters of importance in any uſeful art or ſcience, deſervedly claims the patronage and encouragement of the public; it follows, that whatever improvements are diſcovered in thoſe parts which are moſt beneficial to ſociety in general, demand the moſt ſerious attention.

It is needleſs to inſiſt on the utility of navigation, and its ſubſerviency to the very exiſtence of a commercial nation: theſe are uncontroverted truths, and will remain ſo, while any intercourſe is carried on between the diſtant regions of the globe.

In the following pages, I have endeavoured, by the moſt intelligent methods, to inſtruct the judicious mariner in thoſe parts of navigation, which have hitherto been either not duly attended to, or ſufficiently underſtood.

The aſcertaining a ſhip's place at ſea, in reſpect to her diſtance from the equator, has been ſufficiently done by the meridian altitude of the ſun or a ſtar; but the knowledge of her diſtance from the meridian has been much wanted, as of the greateſt conſequence to seamen, and without which, it is impossible to determine the ship's true place.—I have therefore, in the ensuing work, exemplified in a familiar manner, to the most common capacity, the new method of finding the latitude, by taking two altitudes of the sun; and also, the method of finding the longitude, by taking the moon's distance from the sun or a fixed star: these important points the seaman will find executed so conspicuously, as to render every operation of the like kind free from ambiguity or perplexity; without a multiplicity of tables, which greatly embarrass, instead of facilitating such operations.

How far I have succeeded, is, with all due deference, submitted to your candour, by

My Lords and Gentlemen,

Your obedient humble servant,

J. H. MOORE.

THE

PRACTICAL OBSERVER, &c.

The new METHOD of finding the Latitude at Sea, by taking two Altitudes, either in the Forenoon or Afternoon, having the intermediate Time measured by a Common Watch, with Ease and Accuracy, independent of the Sun's Meridian Altitude.

GENERAL RULES.

TO the Arithmetical Complement of the Logarithm of the Co. Sine of the Latitude by Account, add the Arithmetical Com. of the Co. Sine of the Sun's Declination, call that Sum, The Logarithm Ratio.

From the Natural Sine of the greatest Altitude, subtract the Natural Sine of the least Altitude, and find the Logarithm of their Difference, and write it under the Log. Ratio.

Subtract the Hours and Minutes when the Altitudes were taken, from each other, and Half the Difference call, Half Elapsed Time.

With Half the Elapsed Time enter these Tables, and from the Column of Half elapsed Time take out the Log. answering thereto, and set it down under the Log. Ratio.

Add these three Logarithms together, and with their Sum enter the Tables, in the Column of Middle Time, where, having found the Log. nearest thereto, take out the Time corresponding to it, and put it down under Half the Elapsed Time.

Subtract the Less from the Greater, and the Difference will be the Time from Noon, when the greatest Altitude was taken.

With this Time enter these Tables, and from the Column of Rising, take out the Logarithm corresponding to it; from this Logarithm, subtract the Log. Ratio, the Remainder will be the Logarithm of a Natural Number; which, being found in any common Table of Logarithms, and added to the Natural Sine of the greatest Altitude, will give the Natural Sine of the Sun's Meridian Altitude.

Having the Meridian Altitude of the Sun at Noon, the Latitude is found by the usual Method.

N. B. If the Latitude, found by the above Process, should differ widely from the Latitude by Account, it will be proper to repeat the Operation; using the Latitude last found instead of the Latitude by Account, till the Result gives a Latitude nearly agreeing with the Latitude used in the Computation.

By the Sun's Altitude is always meant the Altitude of the Sun's Centre: For obtaining which, at Sea, the usual, and, indeed, the best Method, is, with a well-adjusted Hadley's Quadrant, to observe the Altitude of his lower Limb above the Horizon of the Sea; which being cleared of the Effects of Refraction, and Dip of the Visible Horizon, as found in the Tables for that Purpose, and the Semi-Diameter of the Sun added thereto, will give the correct Altitude of his Centre.

Suppose the Apparent Altitude of the Sun's lower Limb was observed 48° 58′ above the Horizon of the Sea, the Observer's Eye being elevated 20 Feet above the Surface of the Water, requir'd the correct Altitude of his Centre.

	°	′
Observed Altitude	48°	58′
Refraction		1
	48	57
Horizontal Dip for 20 Feet		4
	48	53
The Sun's Semi-Diameter		16
The Correct Alt. of Sun's Centre	49	9

Here the Refraction and Horizontal Dip are taken in whole Numbers, to save the Trouble of working with Seconds; and is exact enough for finding the Latitude at Sea.

EXAMPLE I.

EXAMPLE I.

Being at Sea in Latitude 46° 50′ North by Account, when the Sun's Declination was 11° 17′, N. at 10H. 2M. in the Forenoon; the Sun's Altitude was 46° 55′, and at 11H. 27M. in the Forenoon; the Second Altitude was 54° 7′. Required the true Latitude, and true Time of the Day when the greatest Altitude was taken.

Times.		
H. M. S.	Lat. 46° 50′ Arith. Co. of Co. Sine	0, 16486
11 27 00		
10 2 00	Dec. 11 17 Arith. Co. of Co. Sine	0, 00847
Ela. T. 1 25 00	Added gives the Log. Ratio	0, 17333
½ ELT. 0 42 30		

The Sun's gr. Alt. at 11H. 27M. is 54° 7′ its Nat. Sine 0, 81021
The Sun's least Alt. at 10H. 2M. is 46° 55′ its Nat. Sine 0, 73036

The Remainder or Diff. of Nat. Sines 7985

Log Ratio.	0, 17333
The Common Log. of the Diff. N. S.	3, 90227
In the New Tables in Col. ½ Ela. Time for 42M. 30S. is	0, 73429
Their Sum is the Log. of Middle Time	4, 80989
	H. M. S.
The H. M. &c. for which by the New Tables is	1 15 30
Subtract Half Elapsed Time	0 42 30
The Diff. is the true Space of Time the Sun had to rise to the Meridian when the greatest Altitude was taken	0 33 00

	H.M.
Time per Watch	11 27
Sub. from	12 00
	00 33

00 33 Finding they agree, the Watch is right.

Enter the Tables with 33M. under Col. of Rising, and you'll find the Log.	3, 01488
From which Subtract the Log. Ratio	0, 17333
The Natural Number of which is 694	2, 84155

To

To the Natural Sine of the greateſt Alt.	0, 81021
Add the Natural Number of the above Log.	694
The Sum is the Natural Sine of the Sun's Meridian Altitude, 54° 48′	81715

	90°	00′	
	54	48	
The Sun's Zen. Diſt.	35	12	By obſerving the Sun's Merid. Alt. the ſame Day the Lat. was found to be 46 30 N.
The Sun's Decl.	11	17	
Lat.	46	29	N.

Note. The Arithmetical Comp. is found by ſubtracting the Logarithmic Sine of any Number of Degrees, &c. from 10,00000.

EXAMPLE II.

Being at Sea in Lat. 47° 19′ N. by Account, when the Sun's Declination was 12° 16′ N. at 10H. 24 M. A. M. per Watch, the Sun's Alt. was 49° 09′, and at 1H. 14M. P. M. his Alt. was 51° 59′. Required the Lat.

	H.	M.	S.				
				Alt.	Nat. S.	Lat. 47 19	0, 16880
	10	24	0	49° 9′	75642	Sun's Dec 12 16	0, 01003
	1	14	0	51 59	78783		
Elap. T.	2	50	0			Log. Ratio	17883
				Diff. N. S.	3141	Its Log.	3, 49707
½ El. T.	1	25	0	Its Log. in Col. of ½ Elap. Time is			0, 44077
Sub.	0	15	0	Col. of Mid. Time correſponding to			4, 11667
True T.	1	10	0	Its Log. in Col. of Riſing is			3, 66542
T. p. W.	1	14	0	Log. Ratio Sub.			0, 17883
Wa. faſt	0	4	0	3066 the Nat. Number of this Log.			3, 48659

N.S. Sun's gr. Alt.	78783	90	00
N.S. S. Mer. Alt.	81849 =	54	56
Sun's Zen. Diſt.		35	4
Sun's Decl.		12	16 N.
Lat. in		47	20 North.

Here the Latitude found by Computation may be relied on, as it differs but one Mile from that uſed in the Operation.

EXAM-

EXAMPLE III.

Being at Sea in Lat. 50° 40' North per Account, when the Sun's Declination was 20° 0' South, at 10H. 17M. A. M. per Watch, the Sun's Alt. was found 17° 13', and at 11H. 17M. A. M. per Watch, it was found 19° 41'. Required the Latitude.

Times.	Alt.	Nat. S.		
H. M. S.			Lat. 54° 40'	0, 19803
			Decl. 20 00	0, 02701
10 17 0	17° 13' =	29599		
11 17 0	19 41 =	33682	Log. Ratio	0, 22504

Ela. T. 1 0 0 Diff. N. S. 4083 Its Com. Log. 3, 61098
½El. T. 0 30 0 Its Log. from Col. ½ Elap. Time is 0, 88430
1 01 0 In Col. of Mid. Time corresponding to 4, 72032
Tr. Ti. 0 31 0 From Noon, its Log. from Col. of Ris. 2, 96067
D.p.W. 0 43 0 Log. Ratio Sub. 0, 22504
W. slow 0 12 0 544 N. Num. of 2, 73563
33682 N. S. greatest Alt.

90° 00'
20 01 34226 N. S. of Sun's Mer. Alt. 20° 1'

Zen. Dist. 69 59
Decl. 20 00 S.

Lat. 49 59 N. But as this Latitude differs 41 Miles from that by Account, it will be proper to repeat the Operation, using the Latitude last found instead of the Latitude by Account.

H. M. S. Latitude 49° 59' 0, 19178
½ Elapsed Time 0 30 00 Decl. 20 00 0, 02701
1 00 00
Log. Ratio 0, 21879
True Time 0 30 00 3, 61098
Time per Watch 0 43 00 0, 88430
H. M.
Watch slow 0 13 00 In Col. Mid. T. 1 0 4, 71407

True Time 0 30 0 Its Log. in Col. ½ Ela. E. is 2, 93223
Log. Ratio 0, 21879

517 Nat. Num. of 2, 71344
33682 Nat. S. great Alt.

Nat. S. Sun's Mer. Alt. 34199 = 20° 00'

Zen.

Zen. Dist.	70	00
Decl.	20	00 S.
The Lat.	50	00 North

The Latitude last found, differing only one mile from that used in the Operation, may be depended on as the True Latitude. Hence it is plain, that the Operation is repeated with very little additional Trouble, but few Alterations being necessary.

EXAMPLE IV.

Being at Sea in the Latitude of 60° 0', North by Account, when the Sun was on the Equator, and consequently had no Declination. at 1H. 0M. P. M. per Watch, his Altitude was 28° 53', and at 3H. 0M. P. M. per Watch, it was 20° 42'. Required the true Latitude.

	Times. H. M. S.	Alt.	N. S.		
				Lat. 60°00' =	0, 30103
				Dec. 00 00 =	0, 00000
	1 00 00	28 53 =	48303		
	3 00 00	20 42 =	35348	Log. Ratio	0, 30103
	2 00 00		12955		4, 11244
½ Elap. T.	1 00 00				0, 58700
	2 00 00				
					5, 00047
T. fr. Noo.	1 00 00				3, 53243
Di. p. Wa.	1 00 00			Log. Ratio	0, 30103
			1703		3, 23140
			48303		

	D. M.	
Nat. S. of Sun's Mer. Alt. 50006 =	30 00	Sun's Mer. Alt.
	60 00	Latitude

The Latitude by Computation, coming the same with the Latitude by Account, shews, that the Latitude by Account was right. From the foregoing Examples, it is plain, that the Operation is the same, whether the Sun hath North or South Declination. And it will be the same whether the Ship is in a North or South Latitude. It is also clear, that when the Sun has no Declination, the Arithmetical Complement of the Log. Co. Sine of the Latitude, is the Log. Ratio.

EXAM-

EXAMPLE V.

July 5. 1770, wanting to go through the 8° N. Channel, among the Maldives, and by Account being in Latitude 7° 20′ N. at 7H. 25M. 40S. P. M. the true Altitude of the Sun's Centre was 22° 30′, and at 10H. 31M. 48S. A. M. it was found 63° 40′. Required the Ship's true Latitude.

	H. M. S.	Alt.	Nat. S.		
Times	10 31 48	63° 40′	89623	Lat. by Ac. 7° 20′	0, 00390
	7 25 40	22 30	38268	D. July 5, 22 48	0, 03533
Elap. T.	3 6 8			Log. Ratio	0, 03923
			51355	Its Log.	4, 71058
½ El. T.	1 33 00	Its Log. in Col. of ½ Elap. Time is			0, 40368
	3 1 30			H. M. S.	
				3 1 30	5, 15349
True T.	1 28 30	Its Log. in Col. of Rising is			3, 86709
T. p. W.	1 28 12			Log. Ratio	0, 03923
Wat. fl.	0 0 18		6726 Nat. Num.		3, 72786
	90 00		89623 Nat. S. gr. Alt.		
Mer. Alt.	74 28				
			96349 N. S. Sun's Mer. Alt. 74° 28′		
Zen. Dist.	15 32				
Decl.	22 48				
Lat. in	7 16 North				

N. B. As the Tables are only calculated to 30 Seconds, the Log. for any intermediate Seconds is found by taking the Difference between Log. the next greater and next less, and say, as 30 Seconds is to that Difference, so is the given Seconds, to the Difference of the Log. or if it be any even Part, take such a Part of the Difference, and apply it to the next less Logarithm.

SECOND OPERATION.

		Lat. 7° 16′	0, 00350
		Dec. 22 48	0, 03533
		Log. Ratio	0, 03883
	H. M. S.		4, 71058
	3 1 30		0, 40308
	1 33 00	3 1 30	5, 15309
True Time	1 28 30		3, 86709
N. S. gr. Alt.	89623	Log. Ratio	0, 03883
	6734 N. Nu. Log.		3, 82826
N. S. Sun's M. Al.	96357 = 74 29	Hence the Lat. in is 7° 17′ N	

The

The Latitude laſt found, differing only one Mile from that uſed in the Operation, it may be taken as the True Latitude; and the Operation is repeated with very little additional Trouble, but few Alterations being neceſſary. Hence it is plain, that if you are miſtaken in the Latitude by Account, yet by repeating the Work two or three Times, making uſe of the Latitude laſt found in the next Operation, it will at laſt diſcover itſelf to be true, by being equal to the laſt Suppoſition, which evidently ſhews the excellency of theſe New Tables.

In the former Examples we have conſidered both Altitudes taken at the ſame Place or Station; but as that is ſeldom the Caſe at Sea, the neceſſary Corrections for any Alteration of Station may be readily made, as follows:

	H.	M.
Suppoſe the firſt Altitude in the Forenoon	10	26
The ſecond Altitude in the Afternoon 2H. 43M.	14	43
Difference of Longitude made is 30 miles W. equal to	0	2
	14	41
	10	26
Subtracted is the Elapſed Time	4	15

If a Ship has been ſailing to the Eaſtward, the above two Minutes muſt be added; but unleſs the Difference of Longitude be conſiderable, it is not worth Notice, as it will make a very inconſiderable Error in the Latitude.

Whenever the Ship ſails or makes towards that Point of the Compaſs which the Sun bears upon, ſhe muſt raiſe the Sun's Altitude as many Minutes as the Miles ſhe has run towards it; that is, the Miles run towards the Sun muſt be added to the firſt Altitude; but if ſailing from the Sun, the ſame muſt be ſubtracted: if they are but few, they are not worth minding; and then the Seaman may make a very good Eſtimation by looking at the Log-board only, who, by that, will be able to aſcertain the Diſtance ſailed to, or from the Sun, between the Obſervations, which will be of ſufficient exactneſs in the Practice of Navigation; and if the Ship makes an Angle with the Sun's bearing, it may be readily found by the Table of Difference of Latitude and Departure, and then either add or ſubtract, according as the Caſe requires; as may be ſeen in the following Examples, which are inſerted for the Benefit of thoſe who require a greater Degree of Accuracy.

EXAMPLE VI.

On the 21ſt of December, 1772, being in a Ship from the Bay of Biſcay, bound to the Engliſh Channel, in a briſk Gale running ging N. E. ¾ E. per Compafs, at the Rate of 9 Knots per Hour, at 10H. 00M. A. M. per Watch, obferved the Sun's Altitude 13° 18' bearing South ¾ E. by Compafs, and at 1H. 40M. P. M. per Watch, the Sun's Altitude again was found 14° 15'. the Latitude by Account being then 49° 17' N. Required the true Latitude.

The Correction to the firft Altitude.

The Time of the firft Obfervation is 10H. 00M. A. M. and of the Second 1H. 40M. P. M. the Elapfed Time is 3H. 40M. and the Rate of the Sailing is 9 Miles per Hour; then fay, by the Rule of Three, as 1H. is to 9 Miles, fo is 3H. 40M. to 33 Miles, the Diftance run in the Elapfed Time.

Again, The Sun's Bearing at the firft Obfervation is South ¾ E. the oppofite Point to which is N. ¾ W. or ¾ Point,
And the Ship's Courfe during the Ela. Time is N. b E. ¾ E. 1¾ Points
So the Angle of Ship's Courfe with the Sun's Bearing is 2½ Points

Now in the Table of Difference of Latitude and Departure, to the Courfe 2½ Points, and Diftance 33, the Difference of Latitude is 29, and the Ship is failing from the Sun; therefore from the firft obferv'd Alt. 13° 18', take 29, the Remainder 12° 49, is the firft Altitude corrected, which is to be ufed in the Operation as follows:

	H. M. S.	Alt.	Nat. S.		
				Lat. 49° 17'	0, 18554
Times.	10 00 00	14° 15' =	24615	Decl. 22 28	0, 03749
	1 40 00	12 49 =	22183		
				Log. Ratio	0, 22303
Ela. T.	3 40 00	Diff. N. S.	2432	Its Log.	3, 38596
½ El. T.	1 50 00	Its Log.			0, 33559
	0 10 00	Time correfponding to			3, 94458
	1 40 00	Its Log. in Col. of Rifing is			3, 97170
				Log. Ratio	0, 22303
	90 00		5606	Nat. Num. of	3, 74867
	17 35		24615		
Zent Dift.	72 25	N. S. M. Al.	30221 = 17 35		
Decl.	22 28				
Lat.	48 57 N.				

But as the Latitude by Computation differs confiderably from that by Account, the Work muft be repeated,

Latitude 48° 57'	=	0, 18262
Decl. 22 28	=	0, 03749
Log. Ratio		0, 22011

 H.

	H. M. S.	Diff. N.S. 2432 Its Log.	3. 38596
	1 50 00	Its Log.	0, 33559
	0 10 00	Time answering to	3, 04166
90 00	1 40 00	Its Log.	3, 97170
17 37		Log. Ratio	0, 22011
Zen. Dis. 72 23		5644 Nat. Num. of	3, 75159
Decl. 23 28		24615	
		30259 N. S. Mer. Alt, 17° 37′	

Tr. Lat. 48 55 N. This Latitude differing only 2 Miles from that used in the Computation, it may be depended upon as the true Latitude.

EXAMPLE VII.

A Ship sailing N. E. ¼ E. by Compass, at the Rate of 9 Knots an Hour, at 0H. 31M. 40S. P. M. per Watch, found the Altitude of the Sun's lower Limb 28° 20′ above the Horizon of the Sea, the Observer's Eye being elevated 20 Feet above the Surface of the Water, and the Sun's Bearing, by Compass, being at the same Time S. by W. and at 2H. 58M. 20S. P. M. by Watch, the Altitude of the Sun's lower Limb was 16° 41′ above the Horizon, the Observer's Eye being elevated as before, and the Latitude by Account, at the Time of the last Observation, being 48° 00′ North, and the Declination 13° 17′ South. Required the true Latitude at taking the last Observation.

First observ'd Alt. of S's lower Limb	28° 20′	Second ditto 16° 41′
Refraction to be subtracted	2	3
Corrected for Refraction	28 18	16 37
Dip of the Horizon subtracted	4	4
App. Alt.	28 14	16 33
Sun's Semi-Diameter added	0 16	0 16
Correct Altitudes of Sun's Centre	28 30	16 49

Correction for the first Altitude.

The Time of the first Observation 0H. 31M. 40S. P. M. of the Second 2H. 58M. 20S. P. M. so the Elapsed Time is 2H. 26M. 40S. the Rate of Sailing is 9 Miles per Hour. Then as 1M. : 9 Miles, :: 2H. 26M. 40S. : 22 Miles, the Distance run in the Elapsed Time.

Again,

Again, The Sun's Bearing at the first Observation is S. by W. the opposite Point to which is N. by E. or 1 Point.
The Ship's Course during the Ela. Time is N. E. ¾ E. or 4 ¾ Pts.
So the Angle of the Ship's Course with the Sun's Bearing is } N.E.bN. ¾E. 3 ¾ Pts.

In the Table of Difference of Latitude and Departure, to the Course 3 ¾ Points, and Distance 22 Miles, the Difference of Latitude is 17 Miles, and the Ship sails from the Sun.

Wherefore first observed Altitude 28° 30′ — 17′ = 28° 13′ the first Correct Altitude to be used in the Operation.

	H. M. S.	Alt.	N. S.		
Times.	0 31 40	28 13	47281	La.by Ac. 48° 0	0, 17449
	2 58 20	16 49	28931	Decl. 13 17	0, 01178
				Log, Ratio	0, 18627
Ela. T.	2 26 40	Diff. N,S.	18350	Its Log.	4, 26364
½ El. T.	1 13 20				0, 50132
	1 46 30				4, 95223
	0 33 10	Its Log.			3, 01925
				Log. Ratio	0, 18627

	90 00	N. S. gr. Alt. 47281	
		687 N. Num. of	2, 83298
Mer. Alt.	28 40		
		N, S, Mer. Alt. 47968 = 28° 40′	
Zen. Dis.	61 20		
Decl.	13 17		
Lat.	48 3 N.		

And as it differs but 3 Miles from the Latitude by Account, it may be taken as the true Latitude.

By the Ship's Course per Compass, is to be understood, it's Course made good, Leeway, if any being first allowed, or the Course, by Compass, corrected for the Leeway only, but not for the Variation. Had the Variation of the Compass been applied, both to the Ship's Course and the Sun's Bearing, it would not have made any Difference in the Operation or Result, as the Angle formed by them, will always be the same, whether they are both estimated by the Compass, or when the Variation is allowed on both.

Having in these Operations obtained not only the true Latitude, but also the true Time of the Day, the true Azimuth is easily determined; and as a tolerable Watch can't be supposed to vary in the Space of one, two, or three Hours, the Azimuth may

may be taken at any reasonable Time afterwards, and the Variation of the Compass ascertained in a very easy and familiar Manner, without the true Latitude.

EXAMPLE.

In the Latitude 51° 30′ N. the Sun's Declination 15° 10′ N. at 2M. past Six in the Afternoon, the Sun's Altitude was 11° 30′. The Sun's true Azimuth is required at that Time.

As the Co. Sine of the Sun's Alt.	78° 30′		9, 99119
Is to the Sine of Hour from Noon	6 2	= 90 30	9, 99998
So is Co. Sine Sun's Decl.	74 50		9, 98460
			19, 98458
			9, 99119
To Sine of true Azimuth 80° 2′ N.			9, 99339

This Method of finding the Latitude is of excellent Use, since there are so many Circumstances at Sea which deny the Opportunity of having the Sun's Meridian Altitude; and as the knowing the true Latitude is of the greatest Consequence, especially in coming into the English Channel, &c. where there are frequent Obstructions of Clouds; every Seaman ought to be ready at determining his Latitude, by this Method, whenever an Opportunity offers, least he should not see the Sun upon the Meridian.

Note. The nearer to Noon the Observations are taken, the better; provided the Elapsed Time be not much less than Half the Interval of Time, when they are both taken on the same Side of Noon, nor much greater than once and half the greater Interval, when taken on different Sides of Noon.

To Rectify or Adjust Hadley's Quadrant.

1. For the Fore Observation.

BRING the index close to the bottom, that the middle of the Vernier's scale stand against o degrees: hold the plane of the instrument vertical, with the arch downwards; look through the right-hand hole in the vane, and direct the sight through the transparent part of the glass to observe the horizon. Now if the horizon line, seen both in the quick-silvered part, and through the transparent part, should coincide, or make one straight line, then is the glass truly adjusted: But if one of the horizon lines stand above the other, slacken the screw in the middle of the lever, backwards or forwards, as there is occasion, until the horizon

rizon lines coincide; fasten the screw in the middle of the lever, and then is the horizon glass adjusted.

2. For the Back Observation.

Turn the button on one side, and set the middle line of the index as many degrees before 0 degrees as is twice the dip of the horizon; on your height above the water (found in the Table following) hold the plane of the instrument vertically with the arch downwards, look through the hole in the vane, and if the horizon line, seen through the transparent slit in the glass, coincides with the image of the horizon, seen in the quick-silvered part of the same glass, then is the glass in its position: If not, slacken the screw pin in the middle of the lever behind the glass, and looking through the vane as before directed, turn the screw at the end of the lever backwards or forwards, as it is wanted, until the horizon line coincides; then tighten the middle screw, and the glass is adjusted. In setting this glass by the opposite horizon, the head should be held a little backwards, not to intercept the light from behind. The horizon seen from behind will be inverted; that is, the water will appear above, and the sky below; and if the two horizon lines cross one another, the instrument is not held upright.

Another Adjustment which ought not to be omitted.

Hold the plane of the Quadrant parellel to the horizon, and the index being brought to the beginning of the arch, if the horizon of the sea, or line of the sea, seen by refraction in the quick-silvered part of the horizon glass, be higher than the same seen directly through the transparent part of that glass, unscrew the nearest screw a little, and screw up the opposite one till the direct and refracted horizons agree; on the contrary, if the refracted horizon is lower than the true one, unscrew the screw farthest from you, and screw up the nearest one till the two horizons agree; and take care to leave both the screws tight, by screwing them up equally if they are slack.

To take the Sun's Altitude with Hadley's Quadrant.

1. By the Fore Observation.

Fix the screens above the horizon glass, using either or both of them, according to the strength of the Sun's rays, by turning one or both of the frames of these glasses close against the plane or face of the instrument; then, the face being turned towards the Sun, hold the Quadrant by the braces, or by either radius, as is found most convenient, so as to be in a vertical position, with the arch downwards; put the eye close to the right-

right-hand hole in the vane, look at the horizon through the transparent part of the horizon glaſs; at the ſame time, move the index with the left-hand until the image of the Sun, ſeen in the quick-ſilvered part, falls in with the line of the horizon, taking either the upper or under edge of the Solar image: ſwing your body gently from ſide to ſide, and if the edge of the Sun uſed be obſerved not to cut, but to touch the horizon line, like a tangent, the obſervation is well made: Then ſhall the degrees on the arch, reckoned from that end next your body, give the Altitude of that edge of the Sun which was brought to the horizon. If the lower edge was obſerved, then 16 Minutes added to the ſaid degrees, gives the Altitude of the Sun's centre; but if the upper edge was uſed, the 16 Minutes muſt be ſubtracted.

2. By the Back Obſervation.

Put the ſtem of the ſkreens into the hole next the horizon glaſs, uſing them as before, according to the ſtrength of the Sun's rays; then the back being turned to the Sun, hold the inſtrument by the radius and brace in a vertical poſition, with the arch downwards; put the eye cloſe to the hole in the vane, look for the horizon through the tranſparent ſlit in the glaſs, with the right-hand move the index until the image of the Sun, ſeen in the quick-ſilvered part of the glaſs, ſtands in the horizon line, ſeen through the tranſparent ſlit, uſing either the upper or under edge of the Sun; ſwing your body gently to the right and left, to try if the Sun's edge runs along the horizon; if it does, the obſervation is well made, and the degrees reckoned from that end of the arch fartheſt from your body, will give the Altitude of that part of the Sun which was obſerved. If the Sun's lower edge was obſerved, then 16 Minutes ſubtracted from the before found degrees, will give the Altitude of the Sun's centre; but if the upper edge was obſerved, then the 16 Minutes are to be added. In either of theſe obſervations, if the Altitude of the centre could be obſerved, there would then be no need of uſing the 16 Minutes.

To find the Sun more eaſily in the horizon, turn your back to the Sun, and look through the vane and glaſs down in the middle of the ſhadow of your head, move the index forwards until the refracted image of the horizon before you is brought down to the place you look on in the glaſs, and the index will then be ſet pretty near to the Altitude, and ſo fitted to find the Sun more readily, either in the fore or back obſervation.

The fore obſervation is moſt convenient, eſpecially in great Altitudes, becauſe there is a much larger ſcope above and below the Altitude wanted, than there is in the back obſervation; which,

which, on account of the obliquity of the ſpeculum and horizon glaſſes, is more contracted in its uſe; and indeed the back obſervations need never be uſed for the ſun where there is a clear horizon forwards, or under the ſun. When this is hazy and ill defined, then it is beſt to uſe the back obſervation, if the horizon is clear that way; and therefore it is proper that the horizon glaſs ſhould be always in readineſs, by having it well adjuſted; which, becauſe the former method is not readily attained by beginners, we ſhall annex another, which is ſomewhat more convenient.

Another way to adjuſt for the back obſervation.

Take the altitude of the lower edge of the ſun, by the fore obſervation, as near to noon as can be, then put the ſcreens into the hole near the ſun, and turning your back to the ſun, and holding the inſtrument properly, taking care not to move the index, look for the horizon line through the tranſparent ſlit of the glaſs, and if the horizon line touches the upper edge of the ſun's image in the glaſs, it is properly adjuſted: If they do not touch, turn the glaſs by the lever behind it, till they do. This operation muſt be done quickly, before the ſun ſenſibly alters in altitude, and may be frequently repeated to make the fore and back obſervations agree.

To take the altitude of a ſtar by Hadley's quadrant.

Look directly up at the ſtar through the vane and tranſparent part of the glaſs, the index being cloſe to the button, then will the image of the ſtar, by refraction, be ſeen in the ſilvered part right againſt the ſtar ſeen through the other part; move the index forward, and, as the image deſcends, let the centre of the quadrant deſcend alſo, to keep it in the ſilvered part, till it comes down in a line with the horizon ſeen through the tranſparent part, and the obſervation is made.

By a back obſervation.

Through the vane and the tranſparent ſlit in the glaſs look directly at the ſtar, at the ſame time, move the index till the image of the horizon behind you, being refracted by the great ſpeculum, is ſeen in the quick-ſilvered part, and meets the ſtar, and the index will then ſhew the degrees of altitude.

Hadley's quadrants have of late been applied to take the neceſſary obſervations for finding the longitude at ſea, it has been found, that ſuch obſervations require a degree of accuracy, which the inſtruments conſtructed in the common way, were not

EXAMPLE II.

January 1, 1774, in lat. 50° 34 S. and long. 55° 40 W. at 2H. 53 ½M. P. M. per watch, the true altitude of the sun's centre was 41° 32. Required the true apparent time, and error in the watch.

	H.	M.	S.
Time at ship	2	53	30
Sh's lo. 55°40 W.	3	32	40
Greenwich ti.	6	36	10
S's dec. Jan. 1,	22	59	17
Ditto ditto 2,	22	53	54
Decr. in 24H.		5	23
Then as 24H. :	5	23	::
6H. 36M. :	1	24,	
Decl.	22°	59′	17″
Sub.dif. in 6h. 36m.		1	24
S's dec. at ship	22	57	43
	90		
Polar dist.	67	2	17
Alt. obs.	41	32	
Zenith dist.	48	28	
Co. lat.	39	26	

Zen. dist.	48°	28′	
Ar. co. co. si. lat.	39	26	0,19710
Ar. co. pol. dis.	67	2¼	0,03586
The sum	154	54¼	
½ Sum	77	28	9,98952
Zen. dist. sub.	48	28	
Difference	29	00	9,68557
Sum of four logs.			19,90805
Si. co. ½ hor. angle	25	54	— 9,95402
		2	H. M. S.
Hor. Ang.	51	48	= 3 27 12
			H. M. S.
The appa. time at noon			3 27 12
Time by watch			2 53 30
Watch slow			33 42

To find the Apparent at Sea, by an Observation of a Star.

HAving carefully observed the star's apparent altitude, which correct by the dip and refraction, find the ship's latitude and longitude by account, at the time of observation, by carrying the reckoning forward to that time, and find the star's right ascension and declination.

From the ship's latitude, and star's correct declination and latitude, find the Co. lat. polar distance and zenith distance, and with these find the hour angle (as shewn in the last examples of the sun) turn this hour angle into time, and apply it to the star's right ascension, by subtracting it when the star is east of the meridian, but adding it when it is west; this gives the right ascension of the mid. heaven.

From

From the right ascension of the mid. heaven (encreased by 24 hours if necessary) subtract the sun's right ascension at preceding noon at Greenwich, taken from page 2d of the month in the ephemeris, the remainder is the apparent time of the observation, nearly at the ship; to which apply the longitude of the ship from Greenwich, turned into time, adding it when the longitude west of Greenwich, but subtracting it when east, and you'll have the apparent time of the observation nearly by the meridian of Greenwich.

Then say, as 24 hours is to the daily variation of the sun's right ascension, so is this time to a number of minutes and seconds, which subtract from the time of observation at the ship, found as above, leaves the correct apparent time at the ship.

EXAMPLE.

Suppose at Sea, May 18, 1774, P. M. in the latitude 33° 43′ and longitude 45° 0′ west of Greenwich by account, the altitude of the bright star in the harp, lyra was observed to be 36° 3′, the height of the eye above the sea being 16 feet. Required the apparent time of observation.

Alt.		36° 3′ 0″	Ship's lat.	33° 43	N.
Dip for 16 feet	3′ 49″		Co. lat.	56 17	
Refr.	1 18	5 7	Lyra decl.	38 35	N.
			Polar dist.	51 25	
True alt. of lyra	35	57 53			
Zen. dist.	54	2 7			

Whence to find the Time.

Co. lat.	56°	17′	Ari. co. si. co. lat.	56°	17′	0,07999
Polar dist.	51	25	Ari. co. si. pol. dist.	51	25	0,10695
Zen. dist.	54	2	Si. ½ sum	80	52	9,99448
Sum	171	44	Si. difference	26	50	9,65456
½ Sum	80	52				
Zen. dist. sub.	54	2	Sum four Logs.			19,83597
Difference	26	50	Si. ½ hor. angle	34	7	9,91798

	2	H. M. S.
Hour angle	68 14 =	4 32 56
Which subtracted from lyra's right ascension		18 29 17
The Rem. is the right ascension of the mid. heaven		13 56 21
From which sub. the sun's right asc. May 18, at noon		3 40 55
Remains the apparent time of ship nearly		10 15 26
Add ship's longitude west of Greenwich,	45° =	3 0 0
Sum is apparent time at Greenwich nearly		13 15 26

Sun's

Sun's right ascension, May 18, at noon, is 3 40 55
Ditto, May 19, 3 44 45

Daily diff. or increase of right ascension 3 59. Then say, As 24H. : 3′ 59″, :: 13H. 15M. 26S. 2′ 13″, which subtracted from 10H. 15M. 26S: the time at the ship leaves 10H. 13M. 13S. the correct apparent time at the ship, at the time of observation.

Note 1. If an observation of the sun has not been taken the preceding noon, or two altitudes to find the latitude, it may be ascertained by taking the meridian altitude of the star, either before or after the observation is made for finding the time.

Note 2. If the ship's longitude east of Greenwich in time be greater than the apparent time at the ship, the apparent time must be increased by 24 hours before subtracting the longitude; and in this case, the sun's right ascension must be taken out of the ephemeris for one day of the month less than that reckoned at the ship. And if the ship's longitude west of Greenwich in time, added to the apparent time of the ship, makes more than 24 hours, 24 hours must be subtracted from the sum, to obtain the apparent time at Greenwich; and the sun's right ascension must be taken out of the ephemeris for one day of the month more than that reckoned at the ship.

The object, whether sun or star, whose altitude is taken for finding the time, must be, at least, three or four points of the compass distant from the meridian; because, near the meridian, the alteration in altitude is too slow for ascertaining the time with proper exactness; but the nearer the object is to the east or west, the better, provided it be not less than 5° high; for as the refraction is variable and irregular near the horizon, less altitudes than 5° ought not to be used, as the effect of refraction upon them cannot be determined with sufficient certainty.

As often as the moon's distance from the sun or star is observed, in order to find the longitude, the apparent time at the ship must be found. The difference between this time, and the time of taking the altitude for finding it, given by the watch, shews the error of the watch, and whether it be too fast or too slow; and this error must be carefully allowed for, in estimating the time of taking the moon's distance from the sun or star. The less the interval of time between finding the apparent time, and observing the moon's distance, the better; and it is the same whether it be before or after observing her distance.

To

To take the Observations necessary for finding the Longitude at Sea.

THE capital observation for this purpose is, that of the distance of the moon from the sun, or some remarkable star not far from the zodiac. In order to make such observation, the observer must be furnished with a watch that can be depended upon for keeping time, within a minute for six hours; and with a good Hadley's quadrant, or rather sextant, which is preferable to a quadrant. The instrument will still be more fit for the purpose if it be finished with a screw, to move the index gradually and steadily; an additional dark glass, lighter than the common screens, to take off the glare of the moon's light, in observing her distance from a fixed star; and a small telescope magnifying three or four times, to render the contact of the star with the moon's limb more discernable; a magnifying glass of 1 ½ or 2 inches focus will assist the observer to read off his observation with greater ease and certainty.

The observer must in the first place, examine his instrument with the greatest care, and adjust it with the utmost exactness possible; which done, let him proceed to his observation as follows.

If the distance of the moon from the sun is to be observed, turn down one of the screens, look at the moon directly through the transparent part of the horizon glass, and keeping her there, gently move the index till the sun's image is brought into the silvered part of that glass, bring the nearest limbs of both objects into contact, and let the quadrant librate a little on the lunar ray, whereby the sun will appear to rise and fall by the side of the moon; in this motion the nearest limbs must be made to touch one another exactly, by moving the index; when this is effected, the observation is made; and the division cut by the vernier scale will shew the distance of the nearest limbs of the objects.

If the distance of the moon from a star is to be observed, when the moon is very bright, turn down the lightest screen, or use a dark glass, lighter than the screens, and designed for this particular purpose; look at the star directly through the transparent part of the horizon glass, and keeping it there, move the index, till the moon's image is brought into the silvered part of the same glass; let the quadrant librate gently on the star's ray, and the moon will appear to rise and fall by the star; between the librations, move the index, till the moon's enlightened limb is exactly touched by the star, then the observation is made.

The quadrant is to be held as for a fore observation, and its plane must always be made to pass through the two objects whose

distance

distance is to be observed, and for that purpose, must be put into various positions, according to the situation of the objects, which will be rendered familiar by a little experience.

At the very instant, or at most within a very few seconds of the time, at which the observer gives notice of compleating his observation, somebody must observe the hour, minute, and quarter minute (if there be no second hand) of the watch, used for finding the apparent time; and at the same instant of the observer's giving the aforesaid notice, or at the utmost within a minute of that time; two assistants must take the altitudes of the two objects, whose distance is observed; all which being done, the observations necessary for ascertaining the longitude are compleated.

In the ephemeris is found, the moon's distance from the sun, and also from proper stars, to every three hours apparent time, by the meridian of Greenwich; and to afford the mariner greater number of opportunities of observation, and means of attaining a greater degree of exactness, her distance is generally set down from at least one object on each side of her. Her distance from the sun is found set down, while it is between 40° and 120, so that by using a sextant, it may be observed for two or three days after her first, and before her last quarter; while she is between 20° and 40° from the sun, her distance is set down only from a star on the contrary side to the sun: while she is between 40° and 90° from the sun, her distance is set down both from the sun and from a star, on the contrary side to the sun; when she is between 90° and 120° from the sun, her distance is set down both from the sun and a star, on the same side with the sun, and also from a star on the contrary side to the sun. Lastly, when she is above 120° from the sun, her distance is set down from two stars, one on each side of her. Her distance from objects on the east of her, is found in the ephemeris, in the 8th or 9th pages of the month; her distance from objects on the west of her, is found in the 10th and 11th pages of the month.

An observer who uses the ephemeris, must observe the moon's distance from some of those stars only, whose distance from her is set down in the ephemeris, and the distances there set down afford him a ready means of knowing the star from which her distance ought to be observed; for he has nothing to do but to set his quadrant to the distance computed roughly at the apparent time, estimated nearly by the meridian of Greenwich, and look to the east or west of the moon, according as the distance at Greenwich is found in the 8th or 9th, or in the 10th or 11th pages of the month, and having found the moon upon the

horizon

horizon glass, let him give a sweep with his quadrant to the right or left, and he will find the star he wants, if it be above the horizon, and the air be clear, nearly in a line perpendicular to the line joining the moon's horns, or which is the same, in the line of the moon's shorter axis produced.

The time at Greenwich is estimated nearly by turning the ship's supposed longitude from Greenwich into time, and adding it to, or subtracting it from, the apparent time at the ship; as the ship is east or west of Greenwich; and the distance of the moon from the star, at this time, is found roughly, by saying, as 180 minutes, the number of minutes in three hours, is to the difference in minutes (neglecting seconds) between this nearly estimated time, and the next preceding time set in the ephemeris; so is the difference in minutes between the distances in the ephemeris, set down for the next preceding time and the next following time, to a number of minutes, which added to, or subtracted from, the distance set down for the said preceding time, according as it is increasing or decreasing, gives the distance nearly at the time the observation is to be made, and to which the quadrant or sextant is to be set.

To reduce the Observed or Apparent Distance, of the Moon's Limb from a Star, or from the Sun's Limb to the true Distance of their Centres, and to find the Longitude of the Ship from Greenwich.

TO the apparent time of the observation at the ship, apply the longitude turned into time, by subtraction or addition, according as the ship is east or west of Greenwich; this gives the apparent time of the observation, which call the *reduced time*.

In page the 7th of the month, in the ephemeris, seek the nearest noon or midnight preceding the reduced time; and also the nearest noon or midnight following it; always taking the nearest to the reduced time, both before and after it, whether noon or midnight.

Write down the moon's semi-diameter, and horizontal parallax, for the preceding noon or midnight, and also for the following noon or midnight; and find the difference between the two semi-diameters, and between the two parallaxes: The first of these differences is the variation of the semi-diameter in 12 hours; and the second, the variation of the horizontal parallax in 12 hours; then say, as 12 hours is to the difference between the reduced time and the preceding noon or midnight, so is the variation of the

the ſemi-diameter in 12 hours to a fourth proportional, and ſo is the variation of the horizontal parallax in 12 hours to a fourth proportional; theſe fourths applied reſpectively to the ſemi-diameter and parallax, for the preceding noon or midnight, by addition or ſubtraction, according as the ſemi-diameter and parallax are increaſing or decreaſing, give the moon's horizontal ſemi-diameter and parallax for the reduced time.

To the moon's horizontal ſemi-diameter for the reduced time, add the correction anſwering to her obſerved altitude, taken from the table; the ſum is the true apparent ſemi-diameter, at the time and place of obſervation.

To the obſerved diſtance of the moon's limb from a ſtar, apply the moon's true apparent ſemi-diameter, juſt found by addition or ſubtraction, according as the limb, neareſt to, or fartheſt from, the ſtar, was obſerved, and you will have the apparent diſtance of the moon's centre from the ſtar. But to the obſerved diſtance of the ſun and moon's neareſt limbs, add the ſum of the ſun's ſemi-diameter, taken from page 3d of the month in the ephemeris, and the moon's true apparent ſemi-diameter juſt found, and you will have the apparent diſtance of their centres.

Take the difference between the ſun's ſemi-diameter found in the ephemeris, and the dip of the horizon, and add it to the obſerved altitude of the ſun's lower limb, but ſubtract from the obſerved altitude of his higher limb, and you will have the apparent altitude of his centre. Take the difference between the moon's true apparent ſemi-diameter and the dip, and add it to the obſerved altitude of her lower limb, but ſubtract it from the obſerved altitude of her higher limb, and you will have the apparent altitude of her centre; and ſubtract the dip from the obſerved altitude of a ſtar, and you will have its apparent altitude.

From the apparent altitude of the ſun's centre, ſubtract the correction to that altitude, taken from the table, and you will have its true altitude; to the apparent altitude of the moon's centre, add the correction to that altitude, and her horizontal parrallax at the reduced time, taken from the table, and you have the true altitude; and from the apparent altitude of a ſtar, ſubtract its refraction, taken from the table, and you will have its altitude.

To the natural co-ſine of the difference of the apparent altitude of the moon and object from which her diſtance was obſerved, apply the natural co-ſine of the apparent diſtance of their centres, by ſubtraction or addition, according as this diſtance is

leſs

less or greater than 90°, and seek the logarithm of the remainder or sum.

To this logarithm add the logarithmic co-sines of the true altitudes of the objects; from this sum subtract the sum of the co-sines of the apparent altitudes; and seek the natural number corresponding to the remainder: the difference between this number and the natural co-sine of the difference of the true altitudes of the objects is the natural co-sine of true difference required.

In the ephemeris among the distances of the objects on the day of observation, seek for this computed distance, and if it be there, the time of observation at Greenwich is at the top of the columns above it; but if the computed distance falls between two distances in the ephemeris, as it generally will, then say, as the difference between the two nearest distances in the ephemeris, is to 3H. so is the difference between the first of these distances and the computed distance to the time, which, added to the time standing over the said first distance in the ephemeris, gives the true time of the observation of the objects by the meridian of Greenwich.

The difference between this time and the time of the observation at the ship, being turned into longitude, gives the ship's longitude from Greenwich, east or west, according as the time at the ship is greater or less than that at Greenwich.

EXAMPLE I.

Being at sea, May 14, 1774, in Longitude 20° 30 west of Greenwich, by account, at 6H. 30 P. M. by a watch regulated before by a good observation of the sun's altitude,* I observed the distance of the sun and moon's nearest limbs to be 45° 51, and at the same instant, two assistants observed; the one, the altitude of the sun's lower limb 5° 8¼' or 30'', the other, the height of the moon's lower limb 42° 18', the height of the eye being 18 feet above the sea. Required the ship's true longitude.

	H. M.
Apparent time at ship	6 30
Ship's long. west of Greenwich by acc. 20° 30'	1 22
Reduced time	7 52

* See page 24.

 In

In the ephemeris for May.

The horizontal parallax for that time is	54′ 11		
Moon's ſemi-diameter for reduced time is		14°	46′
Correction for moon's alt. 42° 18′ from table 1ſt			11
Moon's true apparent ſemi-diameters		14	57
Sun's ditto		15	52
Sum of ſun and moon's ſemi-diameters		30	49
Obſerved diſt. of ſun and moon's neareſt limbs	45°	5	45
Apparent diſtance of ſun and moon's centres	45	36	34

Sun's app. ſemid.		15′	52″	Moon's app. ſemid.		14′	57″
Dip for 18 feet		4	3	Dip for 18		4	3
Diff.		11	49	Diff.		10	54
Ob. alt. ſun's low. limb	5°	8	30	Moon's obſ. alt	42	18	00
Sun's app. alt.	5	20	19		42	28	54
Cor. from table 1ſt		9	16	Cor. from table 2d		38	2
Sun's true alt.	5	11	3	Moon's true alt.	43	6	56
				Sun's true alt.	5	11	3
Moon's app. alt.	42	28	54				
Sun's app.	5	20	19	Diff. true alt.	37	55	53
Diff. app. altitudes	37	8	35				

Nat. co. ſi. diff. of app. alt.	37°	8′	35″	79714	
Nat. co. ſine app. diſtance	45	36	34	69955	
Diff. of nat. Sines				9759 its log.	3,98941
Add { Co. ſine ſun's true alt.	5	11	3	— 9,99822 }	
Sum { Co. ſi. moon's tr. alt.	43	6	56	— 9,86332 } =	19,86154
					23,85095
Sub. { Co. ſi. ☉'s app. alt.	5	20	19	— 9,99811 }	
Sum { Co. ſi. mn's app. alt.	42	28	54	— 9,86774 } =	19,86585
Nat. number to remainder				9663	3,98510
Nat. co. ſine diff. true alts.	37	55	53 =	78875	
Nat. co. ſine true diſt.	46°	12′	5″	69212	

Now

Now in page 8th of the month in the ephemeris, I find that on

May 14,	H.					H.		
Preceding nearest dist. at 6,	45°	18′	0″	pre. near. dist. at 6		45°	18′	0″
following nearest dist. at 9,	46	38	57	Computed dist.		46	12	5
Difference	1	20	57	Difference		0	54	5

then say, by the rule of three, as 1H. 20M. 57S. : 3H. :: 54M. 5S. : 2H. 0M. 15S. which being added to 6 hours, the time standing over the preceding distance, gives 8H. 0M. 15S. the true time of the observation at Greenwich, and the time at ship was 6H. 30M. the difference between these times is 1H. 30M. 15S. this reduced into longitude, by allowing 15° to one hour, gives 22° 34′ the longitude of the ship from Greenwich, and is west because the time at the ship is less than at Greenwich.

EXAMPLE II.

Being at Sea, May 18, 1774, in latitude 33 43 N. and longitude, 45 W. by account, at 10H. 12M. P. M. per watch, I observed the distance of the moon's farthest limb from the star Spica to be 50° 27¾, and at the same time three assistants observed, one the altitude of the moon's lower limb 24° 18′ 40″, another the altitude of Spica 45 13½, and the third, in order to find the apparent time, the altitude of the bright star in the harp lyra 36 : 3½; these observations were made with Hadley's quadrants well adjusted, the height of the eye above the water being 18 feet. Required the ship's true longitude.

The true apparent time at the ship being computed from the bright star's declination, and altitude with the ship's longitude, is found to be (see page 27)

is found to be (see page 27)	10h.	13	13
Ship long. west of Greenwich by acc. 45	3	0	0
Reduced time.	13	13	13

Now as this time is so near midnight, the moon's horizontal parallax and semi-diameter may be taken for that time, as the variation in so short a time after midnight, would not affect the calculation much. Therefore,

May the 18th, the mn's hor. sem. is 15″ 16″ and hor. par. 56′ 4″

Moon's true hor. semi-diameter for reduced time		15′ 16″
Correction from the table 1st for obs. alt. 24° 18′ 40″		7
Moon's true apparent semi-diameter		15 23
Obs. distance of moon's farthest limb from Spica		50 27 45
App. distance of moon's centre from Spica		50 12 22

Spica's

Spica's obſ. alt	45°13'15"			Moon's true ap. ſemi		15	23
Dip for 18 feet		4	3	Dip for 18 feet		4	3
App. alt.	45	9	12	Diff.		11	20
Ref. for that alt.			57	Moon's obſ. alt. low. limb	24	18	40
Spica's true alt.	45	8	15	App. alt. moon's cen.	24	30	0
				Cor. fr. ta. 2d		48	53
Spica's app. alt.	45	9	12	True alt. moon's centre	25	18	53
Moon's app. alt.	24	30	0	Spica's true alt.	45	8	15
Diff app. alt.	20	39	12	Diff. true alts.	19	49	22

Nat. co. ſi. diff. app. alt. 20° 39' 12" — 93573
Na. co. ſi. dif. of mo. & ſtar 50 12 22 — 64003

Diff. nat. ſines				29570 its log.		4,47085
Add { Co. ſi. ſtar's true alt.	45	8	15	9,84844 }	=	19,80459
Sum { Co. ſi. mn's true alt.	25	18	53	9,95615 }		
						24,27544
Sub. { Co ſi. ſtar's app. alt.	45	9	12	9,84836 }	=	19,80734
Sum { Co. ſi. mn's ap. alt.	24	30	0	9,95902 }		
Nat. number of the remainder				29384		4,46810
Nat. co. ſi. diff. true alt.	19°	49'	22"	94073		

Nat. co. ſi. true dif. of moon and ſtar 64689 = 49° 41' 33"

Now in page 10 of the month in the ephemeris, I find that on May 18, H.

The prec. near. dif. at 12 is	50°	16'	13"	Prec. near. dif.	50	16	13
The following near. dif.	48	42	9	Computed dif.	49	41	33
Diff.	1	34	4	Diff.		34	40

Then, as 1H. 34M. 4S. : 3H. :: 34M. : 20S. : 1H. 6M. 20S. which added to 12H. the time ſtanding over the next preceding diſtance, gives 13H. 6M. 20S. the time of the obſervation at Greenwich; the time at the ſhip was 10H. 13M. 13S. the difference is 2H. 53M. 7S.

Then, as 1H. : 15° :: 2H. 53M. 7S. : 43° 16¼, the difference of longitude, which is weſt, becauſe the time at the ſhip is leſs than at Greenwich.

EXAM.

EXAMPLE III.

Suppose May 25, 1775, in longitude 20° E. of Greenwich, by account, at 6H. 30M. P. M. per watch, regulated before by equal Altitudes of the sun; the distance of the sun and moon's nearest limbs was observed to be 44° 57′ 30″; at the same time the altitude of the sun's lower limb was 5° 8½′; and the moon's lower limb 42° 18″; the eye being 18 feet above the surface of the sea. Required the longitude.

	H.	M.
Apparent time of the observation at the ship	6	30
Ship's longitude east of Greenwich, by acc. 20°	1	10
Reduced time	5	20

In the ephemeris, and for the month of May,
In page 3 for the month, the 25th, the sun's semid. is 15′ 49″
In page 7.

May 25th at noon moon's hor. semid.	15′ 42″	Hor. par.	57′ 37″
May 25th at midt. moon's hor. semid.	15 38	Hor. par.	57 22
Variation in 12 hours	0 4		0 15

Then as 12H. : 4″ :: 5H. 20M. : 1″, and because the semi-diameter is decreasing, 15′ 42″ — 1″ = 15′ 41″ = moon's horizontal semi-diameter, at the reduced time.

And as 12H. : 15″ :: 5H. 20′ : 6″, and because the parallax is decreasing, 57′ 37″ — 6″ = 57′ 31″, moon's true horizontal parallax at the reduced time.

Moon's hor. semi-diameter for the reduced time		15′	41″
Correction from table 1st			11
Moon's true apparent semi-diameter		15	52
Sun's ditto		15	49
Sum of the sun and moon's semi-diameters		31	41
Obs. dist. of the sun and moon's nearest limbs	44°	57	30
Apparent distance of sun's and moon's centres	45	29	11

Sun's app. semid.	0°	15′	49″	Moon's true app. semi.	0°	15′	52″
Dip for 18 feet		4	3	Dip		4	3
Difference	0	11	46	Difference	0	11	49
Obs. alt. sun	5	8	30	Obs. alt. m's lo. limb	42	18	00
App. alt. sun's cen.	5	20	16	App. alt. m's centre	42	29	49
Corr. from table 1st		9	16	Corr. from table 2d		40	50
Cor. alt. sun's cen.	5	11	00	Moon's true alt. cen.	43	10	39

Moon's

Moon's app. alt.	42° 29′ 49″	Moon's true alt.	43 10 39
Sun's ditto	5 20 16	Sun's ditto	5 11 00
App. alt.	37 9 33	Diff. of true alt.	37 59 39

Nat. co. si. diff. app. alt. 37° 9′ 33″ — 79693
Nat. co. si. apparent dist. 45 29 11 — 70108

Diff. of natural sines 9585 its log. 3,98159

Add Sum { Log. co. si. ☉'s true alt. 5 11 00 — 9,99822 ; Log. co. si. m's tr. alt. 43 10 39 — 9,86287 } — 19,86109

23,84268

Sub. Sum { Log. co. si. sn's ap. alt. 5 20 16 — 9,99811 ; Log. co. si. m's tr. alt. 42 29 49 — 9,86767 } — 19,86588

Nat. number of the remainder 9480 3,97680
Nat. co. si. diff. of the true alt. 36 59 39 78813

Nat. co. si. true distance 46° 6′ 24″ = 69333

Preceding nearest dist.	44° 59′ 40″	Preceding	44° 59′ 40″
Following	43 27 40	Computed dist.	46 6 24
Difference	1 32 00	Difference	1 6 44

Then as 1° 32′ : 3H. :: 1° 6′ 44″ : 2H. 10M. 22S. which being added to 3 hours, the time standing over the preceding distance, gives 5H. 10M. 34S. the true time of the ship at Greenwich; and the time at the ship was 6H. 30M. the difference between these times is 1H. 19M. 26S. which turned into longitude, gives 19° 50, and is east, because the time at the ship is greater than at Greenwich.

In order to obtain a greater degree of exactness, it will be better to repeat the observation of the same object, till at least three distances, and their corresponding altitudes and times be obtained; but the more they are taken the better, only they must all be included within the space of half an hour; the sum of all the observed distance and altitudes divided severally by the number of observations, gives the mean time, distance, and altitude; and these means are to be used as if they had been obtained by a single observation, and may be depended upon with greater certainty.

Let us for axample take the first example from the nautical ephemeris, in the year 1767, done by Mr. Maskelane, astronomer royal, and by comparing the results, we shall be able to judge of the accuracy of this method.

EXAMPLE IV.

Suppose that at sea, on April 4th, 1767, the distance of the sun and moon's nearest limbs, with the respective altitudes of their lower limbs were observed, as in the margin, the eye being 18 feet above the water, and the ship in latitude 34 17 N. longitude 17 46 W. of Greenwich, by account, the watch not yet regulated. The ship's true longitude at the time of observation is required.

	Times.	Distances sun & moon	Sun's alt.	moon's alt.
	H. M. S.	D. ′ ″	° ′	
	4 47 14	73 41 53	22 50	80 17
	4 50 11	73 43 55	22 12	80 36
	4 55 26	73 47 33	21 6	81 9
Sum	14 33 51	221 13 21	66 8	242 2
Means	4 50 57	73 44 27	22 3	80 41

As the watch was not regulated, the first thing to be done is to compute the apparent time of observation; and the sun being abundantly distant from the meridian, the mean of the three altitudes in the margin may be supposed preferable to any single observation for that purpose: Wherefore to the observed altitude of the sun's lower limb, 22° 3′, and 11′ 58″, (the difference between his semi-diameter found in the ephemeris, 16′ 1″, and the dip on 18 feet, 4′ 3″), the sum 22° 14′ 58″ is the apparent altitude of his centre, from which subtracting 2′ 11″, the (correction to that altitude, taken from table 1st) there remains 22° 12′ 47″, from the sun's true altitude. The time by watch is 4H. 50M. 57S. to which add 1H. 11M. 4S. the longitude by account west of Greenwich in time, and you have 6H. 2M. 1S. for the time of Greenwich estimated nearly; and to this time the declination is found to be 5° 48′ N. From the altitude, declination, and latitude, now all known, the time of the mean of the observation is found to be 4H. 28M. 19S.

Time at ship	4 28 00	Hor. par. at noon	56 24
Long. per acc.	1 11 04	Hor. par. at midt.	56 1 D.
Ap. time at Gree.	5 39 04		23 ½ = 11″dif.
Horizon. semid.	15 19,	hor. par. at redu. time	56 12

horizontal

Horizontal semi-diameter		15 19
		16
Moon's semid.		15 35
Sun's semid.		16 01
Sum		31 36
Distance	73	44 27
App. dist. cen.	74°	16′ 03

Obs. alt. moon's	80 41 00	Observed altitude sun's	22 03 00
Diff. Sem. and dip	11 32	Diff. Semid. and dip	11 58
App. alt. cen.	80 52 32	App. alt. centre	22 14 58
Correction	08 46	Correction	2 11
True alt. centre	80 01 18	True alt. sun's centre	22 12 47
		True alt. moon's centre	81 01 18
Moon's app. alt.	80 52 32		
Sun's app. alt.	22 14 58	Difference	58 48 31
Difference	58 37 34		

Nat. co. si. diff. app. alt.	58 37 34 —	52063	
Nat. co. si. app. distance	74 16 03 —	27114	
		24949 its log.	4,39707
Sum { Co. si. m's true alt.	81 01 18 —	9,19333 }	19,15984
Add { Co. si. s's true alt.	22 12 47 —	9,96651 }	
			23,55691
Sum { Co. si. m's app. alt.	80 52 32 —	9,20027 }	19,16667
Sub. { Co. si s's app. alt.	22 14 58 —	9,96640 }	
Nat. Number to the remainder		24560 its log.	4,39024
Sub. nat. co. si. diff. true alt.	58 48 31 —	51790	
Nat. co. sine true distance	74° 11′ 56″	27230	

Preceding nearest dist.	73 01 27	Prec. nearest dist.	73 01 27
Next nearest distance	74 28 50	Computed distance	74 11 56
	1 27 23		1 10 29

Then say, as 1H. 27M. 23S. : 3H. :: 1H. 10M. 29S. : 2H. 25M. 11S. which added to 3 hours, gives 5H. 25M. 11S. the time at the ship was 4H. 28M. 19S. therefore the difference is 56′ 52″; now as 60′ : 15° :: 56′ 52″ : 14° 13 the longitude

itude required, and is weſt, becauſe the time at the ſhip is leſs than at Greenwich, differing from the longitude found by the aſtronomer royal ¾ of a Mile.

The diſtance of the moon from the ſun, or from a ſtar, well obſerved with a good inſtrument, together with the time of the obſervation, and the altitudes of the two objects, is ſufficient to determine the longitude, with the help of the ephemeris and the preceding method of calculation, always within a degree, and generally nearer; but it will conduce to ſtill greater accuracy, if the obſerver takes the moon's diſtance from two ſtars, or from the ſun and a ſtar, or when the moon is between 90° and 120° from the ſun, and two ſtars, if he can be ſo lucky as to obtain the ſeveral obſervations; obſerving the moon's diſtance from each object, two, three, or more times.

For the longitude being computed from the ſet of obſervations made with each object reſpectively, the mean of the reſults will propably approach nearer to the truth than any one reſult ſeparately. Particularly the moon's diſtance ſhould be taken from an object on each ſide of her, as often as there is opportunity; and the mean of the reſults from hence will probably be as exact again, as either by itſelf, eſpecially ſo far as depends upon any imperfection of the inſtruments, and unavoidable ſmall errors in the uſe of them; for errors of theſe kinds have a natural tendency to correct each other: And in this caſe there will be good reaſon to believe that the true longitude is ſomewhere between the two reſults, or between the extreme reſults, if there are more than two ſets of obſervations.

Suppoſe that at ſea, in latitude 17° 48′ S. longitude 64° 32′ E. of Greenwich, which by account, on September 5, 1767, the diſtance of the moon's fartheſt limb from the ſtar, Pegaſi Markab, with the altitude of the ſtar, and of the moon's lower limb were obſerved, as in the margin, the eye being 12 feet above the water, and the watch not regulated. Required the ſhip's true longitude at the time of obſervation.

	Times.			Diſtances mn. & ſtar			mn's alt.		Star's alt.	
	H.	M.	S.	H.	′	″	°	′	°	′
	14	50	30	44	53	48	15	22	35	22
	14	55	35	44	50	49	14	11	34	15
	15	0	0	44	48	14	13	8	33	17
	15	5	50	44	44	48	11	46	32	1
	15	11	15	44	41	37	10	30	30	50
Sum	75	3	10	223	59	16	64	57	165	45
Means	15	0	38	44	47	51	12	59	33	9

The

The ſtar being at a ſufficient diſtance from the meridian, its mean altitude with the mean time in the margin will ſerve for regulating the watch, or finding the true apparent time without a ſeparate obſervation for that purpoſe.

Wherefore, from the ſtar's mean altitude obſerved 33° 9′, ſubtract the dip for 12 feet = 3′ 18″, and you have the ſtar's apparent altitude 33° 5′ 42″, from which, ſubtracting the refraction 1′ 28″, there remains 33° 4′ 14″, the ſtar's true altitude. The ſtar's declination taken from the table, and fitted to the beginning of September, 1767, is 15° 57′ 34″ N. and from the altitude, declination, now all known; the polar angle or ſtar's diſtance from the meridian is found to be 47° 54′ ½ = 3H. 11M. 38S. The ſtar's right aſcenſion taken from the table, and fitted to the beginning of September, 1767, is 22H. 53M. 13S. to which adding the polar angle 3H. 11M. 38S. becauſe the ſtar is weſt of the meridian, you have 26H. 4M. 51S. the right aſcenſion of the mid. heaven. From this ſum ſubtract the ſun's right aſcenſion for the preceding noon, found in the ephemeris, viz. 10H. 55M. 51S. and there remains 15H. 9M. the apparent time of obſervation at the ſhip nearly, from which ſubtracting 4H. 16M. 8S. the longitude eaſt of Greenwich by account turned into time, you have 10H. 50M. 52S. the apparent time of obſervation by the meridian of Greenwich nearly. Then, as 24H. : 10H. 50M. 52S. :: 3M. 37S. the daily variation of the ſun's right aſcenſion at the given time, 1M. 38S. which ſubtracted from 15H. 9M. leaves 15H. 7M. 22S. the correct time of obſervation at the ſhip.

To 10H. 50M. 52S. the apparent time of obſervation at Greenwich nearly, the moon's horizontal ſemi-diameter is found from the ephemeris to be 16′ 29″, and her horizontal parallax 60′ 32″, add 4 to the ſemi-diameter on account of the altitude 12° 59′, and you have 16′ 33″, the moon's true apparent ſemi-diameter, which, ſubtracted from 44° 47′ 51″, the mean of the obſerved diſtances of the moon's fartheſt limb from the ſtar, leaves 44° 31′ 18″, the apparent diſtance of the moons centre from a ſtar. To the mean of the obſerved altitudes of the moon's lower limb 12° 59′ add 13′ 15″, the difference between her true apparent ſemi-diameter 16′ 33″, and the dip 3′ 18″, and you have 13° 12′ 15″, the apparent altitude of her centre; to which adding 54′ 57″, the correction to that altitude taken from the table, you have 14° 7′ 12″, the true altitude of her centre.

The apparent diſtance of the objects, with the apparent and alſo the true altitude of each of them are now known, from whence computing as before, their true diſtance is found to be 40° 0′ 24″.

In

In the ephemeris, the next preceding diſtance is 45° 6′ 40″, at 9 hours, the next following diſtance at 12 hours 43° 24′ 24″, their difference 1° 42′ 16″, and the difference of the next preceding 45° 6′ 40″, and the computed diſtance 44° 0′ 24″ is 1° 6′ 16″.

Then, as 1H. 42′ 16″ : 3H. :: 1° 6′ 16″ : 1H. 56M. 38S. which added to 9 hours, gives 10H. 56M. 38S. the time of the mean of the obſervation at Greenwich, and the time at the ſhip was 15H. 7M. 22S. The difference 4H. 10M. 44S. = 62° 41′ is the ſhip's longitude from Greenwich, eaſt becauſe the time at ſhip is greater than at Greenwich, differing from the longitude found by the aſtronomer royal ½ a mile.

I cannot quit this ſubject without obſerving another method of determining the longitude at ſea; and though not equal to the former, yet it may ſometimes be practiſed with ſucceſs.

Let the watch be carefully regulated as before directed, either by the ſun or a ſtar. By taking equal altitudes of the moon, find the time of her paſſage over the meridian; take the difference between this time and the next neareſt time of her paſſage over the meridian, found in the ephemeris, and alſo the difference between her paſſage over the meridian the preceding and following days; then ſay, as 24H. : is to this difference, ſo the difference of time between her paſſage over the meridian in the ephemeris, and that by obſervation, to a fourth number, which being applied to the time of obſervation at the ſhip, by addition or ſubtraction, according as the time at the ſhip is more or leſs than that ſet down in the ephemeris, gives the true difference of time between her paſſage over the meridian at the ſhip and Greenwich, which reduced into longitude, gives the longitude eaſt or weſt of Greenwich.

Suppoſe, by taking the mean of three altitudes on the 2d of December, 1775, the moon was found to paſs over the meridian at 9H. 15M. P. M. the watch being well regulated, Required the longitude?

In the ephemeris, and for	H. M.		H. M. S.
Nov. 2, the moon paſſes the mer. at	8 36 P. M.	Moon's paſſage	8 36 0
Nov. 3	at 9 26	Obſerved time at ſhip	9 15 0
Difference in 24 Hours	0 50	Diff. between ſhip and Gre.	39
Then as 24H. : 50M. :: 39M. : 1M. 21S. the difference in 39 Min. add			1 21
True difference of time between ſhip and Greenwich			0 40 21

Then 60M. : 15° :: 40M. 21S. : 10° 5′ the longitude, and is weſt becauſe the time of her paſſage over the meridian at ſhip, is after that at Greenwich. Had the time been before Greenwich time, the 1M. 21S. muſt have been ſubtracted and then the longitude would have been eaſt.

TABLE I.

A Table of Corrections for reducing the moon's femi-diameter to the true femi diameter; and alfo a table for reducing the fun's altitude to the true altitude from the earth's centre.

Apparent Altitude.	Cor. to be added to the moon's app. femi-di.	Cor. to be fubt. from the fun's Altitude.		Apparent Altitude.	Cor. to be added to the moon's femi-diameter	Cor. to be fubt. from fun's altitude.
°	″	′	″	°	″	″
0	0	32	51	45	11	51
1	0	24	20	46	11	49
2	1	18	26	47	12	47
3	1	14	27	48	12	45
4	1	11	42	49	12	43
5	1	9	45	50	12	42
6	2	8	19	51	12	40
7	2	7	11	52	13	39
8	2	6	40	53	13	37
9	2	5	39	54	13	36
10	3	5	6	55	13	35
11	3	4	38	56	13	33
12	3	4	16	57	13	32
13	4	3	54	58	14	30
14	4	3	36	59	14	29
15	4	3	21	60	14	28
16	4	3	8	61	14	27
17	5	2	55	62	14	26
18	5	2	45	63	14	25
19	5	2	35	64	14	24
20	5	2	27	65	14	22
21	6	2	19	66	15	21
22	6	2	12	67	15	20
23	6	2	6	68	15	19
24	7	2	0	69	15	18
25	7	1	54	70	15	17
26	7	1	48	71	15	16
27	7	1	43	72	15	15
28	8	1	38	73	15	14
29	8	1	34	74	15	14
30	8	1	30	75	15	13
31	8	1	27	76	16	12
32	8	1	23	77	16	11
33	9	1	20	78	16	10
34	9	1	17	79	16	9
35	9	1	14	80	16	8
36	9	1	11	81	16	8
37	10	1	9	82	16	7
38	10	1	6	83	16	6
39	10	1	3	84	16	5
40	10	1	1	85	16	4
41	10		58	86	16	3
42	11		56	87	16	3
43	11		54	88	16	2
44	11		53	89	16	1
45	11		51	90	16	0

The corrections of the moon's femi-diameter are the natural fines of her altitude, the radius being 16, which is nearly the moon's mean femi-diameter, and are to be added, becaufe in afcending from the horizon to the zenith, fhe approaches nearer to the obferver by a femi-diameter of the earth, or about one fixteenth part of her diftance from the earth.

The corrections of the fun's altitude are the difference between the refraction at each degree of altitude and his parallax at that altitude, and is to be fubtracted from the apparent altitude.

The corrections are only fet down for degrees, but may be found for any intermediate minutes, by taking proportional parts, or faying as 60 is to the difference between the next greater and next lefs correction, fo is the minutes given to a fourth number, which being fubtracted from the correction of the next lefs altitude, gives the correction required.

Thus the corrections of fun's altitude for 5° 20′ is required.

For altitude 5° the correction is	9′ 45″
6 the correction is	8 19
The difference	1 26

Then, as 60′ : 1′ 26″ :: 20′ : 29, which fubtracted from 9 45, leaves 9′ 16″, the correction for 5° 20″ altitude; or if the third of the difference be taken and fubtracted as above, it will be the fame.

The parallax is the difference between the places in which the fun or moon appear, when feen from any part of the earth's furface; and the places in which they would appear, if feen at the fame time from the earth's centre; or the parallax of the fun or moon is the angle under which the earth's femi-diameter would appear, if feen from the fun or moon. Now as the fun or moon are elevated above their true height by refraction of the atmofphere, fo they are depreffed by their parallax; and as they muft appear higher when viewed from the earth's centre, than they would appear when viewed from the furface thereof: to fave the mariner trouble, the difference is fet down in thefe tables, which applied to the obferved altitude of their centres, gives the true altitudes, as feen from the earth's centre.

The

The Uſe of the following Tables.

THE corrections of the moon's altitude are ſet down only to each degree of altitude, and minute of horizontal parallax; but they may eaſily be found to intermediate minutes of altitude, and ſeconds of horizontal parallax, as follows:

1ſt. When the horizontal parallax is given in minutes without ſeconds, and the altitude in degrees and minutes; for example,

The moon's apparent altitude was 24° 31′, when her horizontal parallax was 59′. Required the correction of her altitude.

Find the correction of altitude for horizontal parallax 59′, and altitude $\left\{\begin{matrix}24^{\circ}\,00\\25\ \ 00\end{matrix}\right\}$ which will be $\left\{\begin{matrix}51'\,47''\\51\ \ 27\end{matrix}\right\}$ and ſubtracting the leſſer from the greater, the difference is 0 20; Then ſay, as 60 : 31′ :: 0′ 20″ : 0′ 10, which ſubtract from 51′ 47″, becauſe the correction for the greater altitude is leaſt, gives 51′ 37, the correction required.

But had the correction for the greater altitude been greateſt, as is the caſe at low altitudes, then the difference 0′ 10″, muſt have been added.

2ndly. When the altitude is given in degrees, and the horizontal parallax in minutes and ſeconds, for example, the moon's apparent altitude was 24°, when her horizontal parallax was 59′ 21″. Required the correction of her altitude.

Find the correction of altitude for altitude 34° and horizontal parallax $\left\{\begin{matrix}59'\\60\end{matrix}\right\}$ which will be $\left\{\begin{matrix}51'\,47''\\52\ \ 42\end{matrix}\right\}$ and ſubtracting the leſſer from the greater, the difference is 0′ 55; then ſay, as 60″ : 21″ :: 55″ : 19″, which added to 51′ 47″, gives 52′ 06″, the correction required.

3dly. When the altitude is given in degrees and minutes, and the horizontal parallax in minutes and ſeconds, for example, the moon's apparent altitude was 24° 31, when her horizontal parallax was 59 21. Required the correction of her altitude.

By laſt caſe, the correction of altitude for horizontal parallax 59′ 21″, and altitude $\left\{\begin{matrix}24^{\circ}\\25\end{matrix}\right\}$ is found to be $\left\{\begin{matrix}52'\,06''\\51\ \ 46\end{matrix}\right\}$ and ſubtracting the leſſer from the greater, the difference is 0 20; then ſay, as 60′ : 31″ :: 0′ 20″ : 0 10, which ſubtracted from 52′ 06″, becauſe the correction to the greateſt altitude is leaſt, gives 51′ 56″, the correction required.

TABLE II.

A Table of the Difference between the Moon's Parallax and Refraction, at each Degree of Altitude and Minutes of Horizontal Parallax.

HORIZONTAL PARALLAX.											
	53	54	55	56	57	58	59	60	61	62	
alt	Corr. ' ''	Corr. ' ''	Corr. ' ''	Corr. ' ''	Corr. ' ''	Corr. ' ''	Corr. ' ''	Corr. ' ''	Corr. ' ''	Corr. ' ''	alt
0	20 0	21 0	22 0	23 0	24 0	25 0	26 0	27 0	28 0	29 0	0
1	28 31	29 31	30 31	31 31	32 31	33 31	34 31	34 31	36 31	37 31	1
2	34 23	35 23	36 23	37 23	38 23	39 23	40 23	41 23	42 23	43 23	2
3	38 20	39 20	40 20	41 20	42 20	43 20	44 20	45 19	46 19	37 19	3
4	41 1	42 1	43 1	44 1	45 1	46 1	47 1	48 1	49 1	50 1	4
5	42 53	43 54	44 54	45 54	46 54	47 53	48 54	49 53	50 53	51 53	5
6	44 15	45 14	40 4	47 14	48 13	49 13	50 13	51 12	52 12	53 12	6
7	45 10	46 16	47 16	48 16	49 15	50 15	51 14	52 14	53 14	54 13	7
8	46 0	46 59	47 59	48 58	49 58	50 57	51 57	52 56	53 55	54 55	8
9	46 33	47 32	48 32	49 31	50 30	51 29	52 28	53 28	54 27	55 26	9
10	46 57	47 57	48 56	49 55	50 54	51 53	52 52	53 51	54 50	55 49	10
11	47 15	48 14	49 13	50 12	51 11	52 10	53 9	54 8	55 7	56 6	11
12	47 27	48 26	49 25	50 24	51 22	52 21	53 20	54 18	55 17	56 16	12
13	47 35	48 34	49 32	50 31	51 29	52 28	53 26	54 25	55 23	56 22	13
14	47 41	48 40	49 38	50 36	51 34	52 33	53 31	54 29	55 27	55 25	14
15	47 42	48 40	49 38	50 36	51 34	52 32	53 30	54 28	55 26	56 24	15
16	47 40	48 38	49 35	50 33	51 31	52 28	53 26	54 24	55 21	56 19	16
17	47 37	48 34	49 32	50 29	51 27	52 24	53 21	54 19	55 16	56 13	17
18	47 31	48 28	49 25	50 22	51 19	52 16	53 13	54 10	55 7	56 4	18
19	47 23	48 20	49 16	50 13	51 10	52 6	53 3	54 0	54 57	55 53	19
20	47 13	48 10	49 6	50 2	50 59	51 55	52 52	53 48	54 44	55 41	20
21	47 2	47 58	48 58	49 50	50 47	51 42	52 38	53 38	54 30	55 20	21
22	46 48	47 44	48 40	49 35	50 31	51 27	52 22	53 18	54 13	55 9	22
23	46 33	47 29	48 24	49 19	50 14	51 10	52 5	53 0	53 55	34 51	23
24	46 18	47 13	48 8	49 2	49 57	50 52	51 47	52 42	53 37	54 32	24
25	46 0	46 55	47 49	48 44	49 38	50 32	51 27	52 21	53 15	54 10	25
26	45 48	46 36	47 30	48 24	49 18	50 12	51 6	52 0	52 54	53 48	26
27	45 22	46 19	47 9	48 3	48 56	49 50	50 43	51 37	52 30	53 24	27
28	45 3	45 54	46 47	47 40	48 33	49 26	50 19	51 12	52 5	52 58	28
29	44 39	45 32	46 24	47 17	48 9	49 2	49 56	50 47	51 39	52 32	29
30	44 16	45 8	46 0	46 52	47 44	48 36	49 28	50 20	51 11	52 3	30
31	43 52	44 43	45 34	46 25	47 17	40 8	49 0	49 51	50 43	51 34	31
32	43 26	44 17	45 8	45 58	46 49	47 40	48 31	49 22	50 13	51 4	32
33	42 59	43 50	44 40	45 30	46 21	47 11	48 1	48 52	49 42	50 32	33
34	42 32	43 22	44 12	45 2	45 51	46 41	47 31	48 21	49 10	50 0	34
35	42 4	42 53	43 42	44 31	45 21	46 10	46 50	47 49	48 37	40 26	35
36	41 35	42 23	43 12	44 0	44 49	45 37	46 26	47 14	48 3	48 52	36
37	41 4	41 52	42 40	43 28	44 16	45 4	45 52	46 39	47 27	48 15	37
38	40 32	41 20	42 7	42 55	43 42	44 29	45 17	46 4	46 51	47 39	38
39	40 1	40 48	41 35	42 21	43 8	43 54	44 41	45 28	46 14	47 1	39
40	39 28	40 14	41 0	41 46	42 32	43 18	44 4	44 50	45 36	46 22	40
41	38 55	39 40	40 26	41 14	41 56	42 41	43 27	44 12	44 58	45 43	41
42	38 20	39 5	39 49	40 34	41 19	42 3	42 48	43 32	44 17	45 2	42
43	37 45	38 29	39 12	39 56	40 40	41 24	42 8	42 52	43 36	44 20	43
44	37 8	37 52	38 35	39 18	40 2	40 44	41 27	42 11	42 54	43 37	44
45	36 32	37 14	37 55	38 29	30 39	40 0	40 46	41 20	42 11	42 53	45

A Table of the difference between the Moon's Parallax and Refraction at each Degree of Altitude and Minutes of Horizontal Parallax.

CORRECTION of the MOON's ALTITUDE.

	HORIZONTAL PARALLAX.										
	53	54	55	56	57	58	59	60	61	62	
alt	Corr. ′ ″	Corr. ′ ″	Corr. ′ ″	Corr. ′ ″	Corr. ′ ″	Corr. ′ ″	Corr. ′ ″	Corr. ′ ″	Corr. ′ ″	Corr. ′ ″	alt
45	36 32	37 14	37 56	38 39	39 21	40 4	40 46	41 29	42 11	42 53	45
46	35 54	36 35	37 17	37 59	38 41	39 22	40 04	40 46	41 27	42 9	46
47	35 16	35 57	36 38	37 19	37 59	38 40	39 21	40 2	40 43	41 24	47
48	34 37	35 17	35 57	36 37	37 17	37 58	38 38	39 18	39 58	40 38	48
49	33 57	34 37	35 16	35 55	36 35	37 14	37 55	38 33	29 12	39 52	49
50	33 16	33 55	34 34	35 12	35 51	36 30	37 8	37 46	38 25	30 3	50
51	32 35	33 13	33 51	34 29	35 0	35 44	36 24	37 0	37 57	30 15	51
52	31 54	32 31	33 8	33 45	34 22	34 58	31 35	36 12	36 49	37 26	52
53	31 11	31 47	32 23	32 59	33 36	34 12	34 48	35 24	36 0	36 36	53
54	39 28	31 3	31 39	32 14	32 49	33 24	34 0	34 35	35 10	35 46	54
55	29 44	30 19	30 53	31 28	32 2	32 36	33 11	33 45	34 30	34 54	55
56	29 0	29 34	37 7	30 41	31 14	31 40	32 21	32 55	33 29	34 2	56
57	28 15	28 48	29 20	29 53	30 26	30 58	31 31	32 4	32 36	33 9	57
58	27 30	28 2	28 34	29 6	29 37	30 9	30 41	31 13	31 44	32 16	58
59	26 44	17 15	27 46	28 17	28 47	29 16	29 49	30 20	30 51	31 22	59
60	25 57	26 27	26 57	27 27	27 57	28 27	28 57	29 27	29 57	30 28	60
61	25 10	25 39	26 8	26 37	27 6	27 35	28 4	28 34	29 3	29 30	61
62	24 23	24 31	25 19	25 47	26 16	26 44	27 12	27 40	28 8	28 36	62
63	23 35	24 2	24 29	24 56	25 23	25 51	26 18	26 41	27 13	27 40	63
64	22 46	23 12	23 39	24 5	24 31	24 58	25 24	25 50	26 17	26 43	64
65	21 58	22 23	22 49	23 14	23 39	24 5	24 30	24 55	25 21	25 46	65
66	21 9	21 33	21 37	22 22	22 46	23 10	23 35	23 59	24 24	24 48	66
67	20 19	20 42	21 5	21 29	21 52	22 16	22 39	23 3	23 26	23 50	67
68	19 28	19 51	20 13	20 36	20 58	21 21	21 43	22 6	22 28	22 51	68
69	18 38	18 59	19 21	19 42	20 4	20 25	20 47	21 8	21 30	21 51	69
70	17 47	18 7	18 28	18 48	19 8	19 24	19 50	20 11	20 31	20 52	70
71	16 30	17 16	17 35	17 55	18 14	18 34	10 15	19 13	19 33	19 52	71
72	16 5	16 23	16 42	17 0	17 19	17 37	17 56	18 14	18 33	18 52	72
73	15 13	15 30	15 48	16 5	16 23	16 40	16 58	17 16	17 33	17 51	73
74	14 21	14 37	14 54	15 10	15 27	15 43	16 0	16 16	16 33	16 49	74
75	13 28	13 44	13 50	14 15	14 37	14 46	15 1	15 17	15 32	15 48	75
76	12 35	12 50	13 4	13 19	13 33	13 48	14 2	14 17	14 31	14 40	76
77	11 42	11 56	12 9	12 23	12 36	11 5	13 3	13 17	13 30	13 44	77
78	10 40	11 2	11 14	11 27	11 29	11 52	12 4	12 16	12 29	12 41	78
79	9 56	10 7	10 19	10 30	10 42	10 53	11 4	11 16	11 27	11 39	79
80	9 2	9 13	9 23	9 32	9 44	9 54	10 5	10 15	10 26	10 36	80
81	8 8	8 18	8 27	8 37	8 46	8 55	9 5	9 24	9 34	9 33	81
82	7 15	7 23	7 31	7 40	7 48	7 56	8 5	8 13	8 21	8 30	82
83	6 21	6 28	6 35	6 42	6 50	6 57	7 4	7 12	7 19	7 26	83
84	5 26	5 33	5 39	5 45	5 51	5 58	6 4	6 10	6 17	6 23	84
85	4 32	4 37	4 42	4 48	4 52	4 58	5 4	5 9	5 14	5 19	85
86	3 38	3 42	3 46	3 50	3 55	3 59	4 3	4 7	4 11	4 15	86
87	2 43	2 47	2 50	2 53	2 56	2 59	3 2	3 5	3 9	3 12	87
88	1 49	1 51	1 53	1 55	1 57	1 59	2 2	2 4	2 6	2 8	88
89	0 55	0 56	0 57	0 58	0 59	1 0	1 1	1 2	1 3	1 4	89
90	0 0	0 0	0 0	0 0	0 0	0 0	0 0	0 0	0 0	0 0	90

TABLE III.

For reducing the Degrees, Minutes, and Seconds of Longitude, *or right* Ascension, *into Hours, Minutes, and Seconds of* Time, *and the contrary.*

Deg.	H.	M.	Deg.	H.	M.	Degrees.	Hours.	
Min.	M.	S.	Min.	M.	S.			
Sec.	S.	T.	Sec.	S.	T.			
1	0	4	31	2	4	70	4	40
2	0	8	32	2	8	80	5	20
3	0	12	33	2	12	90	6	0
4	0	16	34	2	16	100	6	40
5	0	20	35	2	20	110	7	20
6	0	24	36	2	24	120	8	0
7	0	28	37	2	28	130	8	40
8	0	32	38	2	32	140	9	20
9	0	36	39	2	36	150	10	0
10	0	40	40	2	40	160	10	40
11	0	44	41	2	44	170	11	20
12	0	48	42	2	48	180	12	0
13	0	52	43	2	52	190	12	40
14	0	56	44	2	56	200	13	20
15	1	0	45	3	0	210	14	0
16	1	4	46	3	4	220	14	40
17	1	8	47	3	8	230	15	20
18	1	12	48	3	12	240	16	0
19	1	16	49	3	16	250	16	40
20	1	20	50	3	20	260	17	20
21	1	24	51	3	24	270	18	0
22	1	28	52	3	28	280	18	40
23	1	32	53	3	32	290	19	20
24	1	36	54	3	36	300	20	0
25	1	40	55	3	40	310	20	40
26	1	44	56	3	44	320	21	20
27	1	48	57	3	48	330	22	0
28	1	52	58	3	52	340	22	40
29	1	56	59	3	56	350	23	20
30	2	0	60	4	0	360	24	0

The Use of this Table is easy by the Example following. Let it be required to find what Time is required for the Motion of 108° 4' 45'' under the Meridian?

Then against 100°	is	6h	40'	0''
8°	—	0	32	0
4'	—	0	0	16
45''	—	0	0	3
The Answer is	—	7	12	19

M	S	½ Elapf. Time.	Middle Time.	Rising.	M	S	½ Elapf. Time.	Middle Time.	Rising.
0	30	2.66121	2.63982	9.37654 } Co. ar.	30	30	0.87717	4.42386	2.94656
1	00	2.36018	2.94085	97860 } Co. ar.	31	00	87015	43088	96067
1	30	2.18409	3.11694	0.33078	31	30	86324	43779	97456
2	00	2.05916	24187	58066	32	00	85644	44459	98810
2	30	1.96225	31878	77448	32	30	84976	45127	3.00164
3	00	88307	41796	93284	33	00	84317	45786	01489
3	30	81613	48490	1.06673	33	30	83669	46434	02792
4	00	75814	54289	18271	34	00	83030	47073	04077
4	30	70700	59403	28502	34	30	82400	47703	05342
5	00	66125	63978	37653	35	00	81780	48323	06590
5	30	1.61986	3.68117	1.45031	35	30	0.81169	4.48934	3.07819
6	00	58208	71895	53488	36	00	80567	49536	09032
6	30	54733	75370	60440	36	30	79973	50130	10227
7	00	51515	78588	66877	37	00	79387	50716	11406
7	30	48520	81583	72869	37	30	78809	51294	12570
8	00	45718	84385	78474	38	00	78239	51864	13718
8	30	43086	87017	83739	38	30	77677	52426	14850
9	00	40605	89498	88703	39	00	77122	52981	15969
9	30	38258	91845	93399	39	30	76574	53529	17073
10	00	36032	94071	97854	40	00	76033	54070	18162
10	30	1.33915	3.96188	2.02091	40	30	0.75499	4.54604	3.19238
11	00	31896	94207	06131	41	00	74972	55131	20301
11	30	29967	4.00136	09991	41	30	74451	55652	21351
12	00	28120	01983	13887	42	00	73937	56166	22389
12	30	26349	03754	17732	42	30	73429	56674	23414
13	00	24647	05456	20638	43	00	72926	57176	24427
13	30	23010	07093	23915	43	30	72430	57673	25428
14	00	21432	08671	27078	44	00	71940	58163	26418
14	30	19910	10193	30120	44	30	71455	58648	27396
15	00	18440	11663	33063	45	00	70976	59127	28363
15	30	1.17018	4.13085	2.35910	45	30	0.70503	4.59600	3.29320
16	00	15642	14461	38667	46	00	70034	60069	30266
16	30	14307	15796	41338	46	30	69571	60532	31202
17	00	13013	17090	43930	47	00	69113	60990	32128
17	30	11757	18346	46447	47	30	68660	61443	33044
18	00	10536	19567	48893	48	00	68212	61891	33950
18	30	09348	20755	51271	48	30	67769	62334	34847
19	00	08193	21910	53586	49	00	67330	62773	35734
19	30	07067	23036	55841	49	30	66896	63207	36613
20	00	05970	24133	58039	50	00	66466	63637	37482
20	30	1.04901	4.25202	2.60184	50	30	0.66041	4.64062	3.38343
21	00	03857	26246	62274	51	00	65620	64483	39195
21	30	02838	27265	64316	51	30	65204	64899	40039
22	00	01843	28260	66312	52	00	64791	65312	40875
22	30	00870	29233	68262	52	30	64383	65720	41702
23	00	0.99918	30185	70170	53	00	63978	66125	42523
23	30	98988	31115	72036	53	30	63578	66525	43334
24	00	98077	32026	73863	54	00	63181	66922	44138
24	30	97184	32919	75652	54	30	62789	67314	44935
25	00	96310	33793	77505	55	00	62400	67703	45724
25	30	0.95454	4.34649	2.79124	55	30	0.62014	4.68089	3.46507
26	00	94614	35489	80809	56	00	61632	68471	47282
26	30	93791	36312	82461	56	30	61254	68849	48058
27	00	92982	37121	84083	57	00	60879	69224	48811
27	30	92189	37914	85675	57	30	60508	69595	49566
28	00	91411	38692	87238	58	00	60140	69963	50314
28	30	90646	39457	88773	58	30	59775	70328	51056
29	00	89894	40209	90282	59	00	59414	70689	51791
29	30	89156	40947	91765	59	30	59056	71047	52520
30	00	88430	41673	93223	60	00	58700	71403	53243

M	S	Elapf. Time.	Middle Time.	Rising.	M	S	Elapf. Time.	Middle Time.	Rising.
00	30	0.58348	4.72755	3.53959	30	30	0.41488	4.88615	3.88625
01	00	57999	72104	54670	31	00	41261	88842	89097
01	30	57653	72450	55375	31	30	41036	89067	89567
02	00	57310	72793	56074	32	00	40812	89291	90034
02	30	56970	73133	56767	32	30	40590	89513	90498
03	00	56633	73470	57455	33	00	40368	89734	90960
03	30	56298	73805	58137	33	30	40149	89954	91420
04	00	55966	74137	58814	34	00	39930	90173	91876
04	30	55637	74466	59486	34	30	39713	90390	92331
05	00	55311	74792	60152	35	00	39497	90606	92782
05	30	0.54987	4.75116	3.60813	35	30	0.39282	4.90821	3.93232
06	00	54666	75437	61469	36	00	39069	91034	93679
06	30	54347	75756	62120	36	30	38856	91247	94123
07	00	54031	76072	62766	37	00	38646	91457	94566
07	30	53718	76385	63407	37	30	38436	91667	95005
08	00	53406	76697	64043	38	00	38227	91876	95443
08	30	53097	77005	64675	38	30	38020	92083	95878
09	00	52791	77312	65302	39	00	37814	92289	96311
09	30	52487	77616	65924	39	30	37609	92494	96742
10	00	52186	77917	66542	40	00	37405	92698	97170
10	30	0.51886	4.78217	3.67156	40	30	0.37203	4.92900	3.97597
11	00	51589	78514	67765	41	00	37001	93102	98021
11	30	51294	78809	68369	41	30	36801	93302	98443
12	00	51002	79101	68969	42	00	36602	93501	98862
12	30	50711	79392	69566	42	30	36403	93700	99280
13	00	50423	79680	70158	43	00	36206	93897	99696
13	30	50137	79966	70745	43	30	36011	94092	4.00109
14	00	49852	80251	71329	44	00	35816	94287	00521
14	30	49570	80533	71909	44	30	35622	94481	00930
15	00	49290	80813	72485	45	00	35429	94673	01337
15	30	0.49012	4.81091	3.73057	45	30	0.35238	4.94865	4.01743
16	00	48736	81367	73625	46	00	35047	95056	02146
16	30	48461	81642	74189	46	30	34858	95245	02547
17	00	48189	81914	74750	47	00	34669	95434	02947
17	30	47919	82184	75307	47	30	34482	95621	03344
18	00	47650	82453	75860	48	00	34295	95808	03740
18	30	47384	82719	76409	48	30	34110	95993	04134
19	00	47119	82984	76955	49	00	33925	96178	04526
19	30	46856	83247	77498	49	30	33742	96361	04916
20	00	46595	83508	78037	50	00	33559	96544	05304
20	30	0.46335	4.83768	3.78573	50	30	0.33378	4.96725	4.05690
21	00	46078	84025	79105	51	00	33197	96906	06074
21	30	45822	84281	79634	51	30	33018	97085	06457
22	00	45567	84536	80159	52	00	32839	97264	06838
22	30	45315	84788	80682	52	30	32661	97442	07217
23	00	45064	85039	81202	53	00	32485	97618	07595
23	30	44815	85288	81717	53	30	32309	97794	07970
24	00	44567	85536	82230	54	00	32134	97969	08344
24	30	44321	85782	82739	54	30	31960	98143	08716
25	00	44077	86026	83246	55	00	31787	98316	09087
25	30	0.43834	3.86269	3.83749	55	30	0.31614	4.98489	4.09456
26	00	43592	86511	84250	56	00	31443	98660	09823
26	30	43353	86750	84748	56	30	31272	98831	10188
27	00	43114	86989	85242	57	00	31103	99000	10552
27	30	42878	87225	85734	57	30	30934	99169	10914
28	00	42642	87461	86223	58	00	30766	99337	11275
28	30	42409	87694	86709	58	30	30599	99504	11634
29	00	42176	87927	87192	59	00	30433	99670	11992
29	30	41945	88158	87672	59	30	30268	99835	12348
30	00	41716	88387	88150	60	00	30103	5.00000	12703

M	S	Elapf. Time.	Middle Time	Rising.	M	S	Elapf. Time.	Middle Time.	Rising.
00	30	0.29939	5.00164	4.13055	30	30	0.21438	5.08671	4.31801
01	00	29776	00327	13406	31	00	21306	08794	32079
01	30	29614	00489	13756	31	30	21187	08916	32355
02	00	29453	00650	14104	32	00	21066	09037	32631
02	30	29293	00810	14451	32	30	20945	09158	32906
03	00	29133	00970	14797	33	00	20824	09279	33180
03	30	28974	01129	15140	33	30	20704	09399	33452
04	00	28816	01287	15483	34	00	20585	09518	33724
04	30	28659	01444	15824	34	30	20466	09637	33995
05	00	28502	01601	16163	35	00	20348	09755	34265
05	30	0.28346	5.01757	4.16501	35	30	0.20230	5.09873	4.34534
06	00	28191	01912	16838	36	00	20113	09990	34802
06	30	28037	02066	17173	36	30	19996	10107	35069
07	00	27884	02219	17507	37	00	19880	10223	35335
07	30	27731	02372	17839	37	30	19764	10339	35600
08	00	27579	02524	18171	38	00	19648	10454	35865
08	30	27428	02675	18500	38	30	19534	10569	36128
09	00	27277	02826	18829	39	00	19420	10683	36391
09	30	27127	02976	19156	39	30	19306	10797	36652
10	00	26978	03125	19482	40	00	19193	10910	36913
10	30	0.26830	5.03273	4.19806	40	30	0.19080	5.11023	4.37173
11	00	26682	03421	20129	41	00	18968	11135	37432
11	30	26535	03568	20451	41	30	18857	11246	37690
12	00	26389	03714	20771	42	00	18746	11357	37948
12	30	26244	03859	21091	42	30	18635	11468	38204
13	00	26099	04004	21409	43	00	18525	11578	38460
13	30	25955	04148	21725	43	30	18415	11688	38714
14	00	25811	04292	22041	44	00	18306	11797	38968
14	30	25668	04435	22355	44	30	18197	11906	39221
15	00	25526	04577	22668	45	00	18089	12014	39473
15	30	0.25385	5.04718	4.22980	45	30	0.17981	5.12122	4.39724
16	00	25244	04859	23290	46	00	17874	12229	39975
16	30	25104	04999	23599	46	30	17767	12336	40225
17	00	24964	05139	23907	47	00	17660	12443	40474
17	30	24825	05278	24214	47	30	17554	12549	40722
18	00	24687	05416	24520	48	00	17449	12654	40969
18	30	24550	05553	24825	48	30	17344	12759	41216
19	00	24413	05690	25128	49	00	17239	12864	41461
19	30	24277	05826	25430	49	30	17135	12968	41706
20	00	24141	05962	25731	50	00	17031	13071	41950
20	30	0.24006	5.06097	4.26031	50	30	0.16928	5.13174	4.42193
21	00	23871	06232	26330	51	00	16826	13277	42435
21	30	23738	06365	26628	51	30	16724	13379	42677
22	00	23605	06498	26924	52	00	16622	13481	42918
22	30	23472	06631	27220	52	30	16520	13583	43158
23	00	23340	06763	27514	53	00	16419	13684	43398
23	30	23209	06894	27807	53	30	16319	13784	43636
24	00	23078	07025	28099	54	00	16219	13884	43874
24	30	22948	07155	28391	54	30	16119	13984	44111
25	00	22819	07284	28681	55	00	16020	14083	44384
25	30	0.22690	5.07413	4.28969	55	30	0.15922	5.14182	4.44583
26	00	22561	07542	29257	56	00	15823	14280	44818
26	30	22433	07670	29544	56	30	15725	14378	45052
27	00	22306	07797	29830	57	00	15627	14476	45286
27	30	22180	07923	30115	57	30	15530	14573	45518
28	00	22054	08049	30398	58	00	15434	14669	45750
28	30	21928	08175	30681	58	30	15338	14765	45981
29	00	21803	08300	30963	59	00	15242	14861	46212
29	30	21679	08424	31244	59	30	15146	14957	46442
30	00	21555	08548	31523	60	00	15051	15052	46671

M	S.	½ Elapſ. Time.	Middle Time.	Riſing.	M	S	½ Elapſ. Time.	Middle Time.	Riſing.
00	30	0.14957	5.15146	4.46899	30	30	0.09981	5.20122	4.59436
01	00	14863	15247	47127	31	00	09909	20194	59627
01	30	14769	15334	47354	31	30	09837	20266	59818
02	00	14676	15427	47580	32	00	09766	20338	60008
02	30	14583	15520	47806	32	30	09694	20409	60198
93	00	14490	15613	48031	33	00	09623	20480	60388
03	30	14398	15705	48255	33	30	09552	20551	60577
04	00	14306	15797	48479	34	00	09482	20621	60765
04	30	14215	15888	48702	34	30	09412	20691	60952
05	00	14124	15979	48924	35	00	09342	20761	61139
05	30	0.14034	5.16069	4.49145	35	30	0.09273	5.20830	4.61326
06	00	13944	16159	49366	36	00	09204	20899	61512
06	30	13854	16249	49586	36	30	09135	20968	61698
07	00	13765	16338	49806	37	00	09067	21036	61883
07	30	13676	16427	50025	37	30	08999	21104	62068
08	00	13587	16516	50243	38	00	08931	21172	62252
08	30	13499	16604	50460	38	30	08864	21239	62436
09	00	13411	16692	50677	39	00	08797	21306	62619
09	30	13324	16779	50893	39	30	08730	21373	62801
10	00	13237	16866	51109	40	00	08664	21439	62984
10	30	0.13150	5.16953	4.51324	40	30	0.08597	5.21505	4.63166
11	00	13064	17039	51539	41	00	08531	21571	63347
11	30	12971	17125	51753	41	30	08466	21637	63528
12	00	12893	17210	51966	42	00	08401	21702	63708
12	30	12808	17295	52178	42	30	08336	21767	63888
13	00	12723	17380	52390	43	00	08271	21832	64067
13	30	12638	17465	52601	43	30	08207	21896	64246
14	00	12554	17549	52812	44	00	08143	21960	64425
14	30	12474	17633	53022	44	30	08079	22023	64603
15	00	12487	17716	53231	45	00	08015	22088	64780
15	30	0.18304	5.17799	4.53440	45	30	0.07952	5.22151	4.64957
16	00	12222	17881	53648	46	00	07889	22214	65134
16	30	12140	17963	53856	46	30	07827	22276	65310
17	00	12058	18045	54063	47	00	07765	22338	65486
17	30	11977	18126	54269	47	30	07703	22400	65661
18	00	11896	18207	54475	48	00	07641	22462	65836
18	30	11815	18288	54680	48	30	07579	22524	66010
19	00	11734	18369	54885	49	00	07518	22585	66184
19	30	11654	18449	55089	49	30	07457	22646	66357
20	00	11574	18529	55293	50	00	07397	22707	66539
20	30	0.11495	5.18608	4.55496	50	30	0.07337	5.22766	4.66702
21	00	11416	18687	55698	51	00	07277	22826	66874
21	30	11337	18766	55900	51	30	07217	22886	67046
22	00	11259	18844	56101	52	00	07158	22945	67217
22	30	11181	18922	56301	52	30	07099	23004	67388
23	00	11104	18999	56501	53	00	07040	23062	67558
23	30	11027	19076	56701	53	30	06981	23123	67728
24	00	10950	19153	56900	54	00	06923	23180	67897
24	30	10873	19230	57098	54	30	06865	23238	68066
25	00	10797	19306	57296	55	00	06808	23295	68235
25	30	0.10721	5.19382	4.57494	55	30	0.06751	5.23352	4.68403
26	00	10645	19458	57690	56	00	06694	23409	68571
26	30	10570	19533	57886	56	30	06637	23466	68738
27	00	10495	19608	58082	57	00	06580	23523	68905
27	30	10421	19682	58277	57	30	06524	23579	69072
28	00	10347	19756	58472	58	00	06468	23635	69237
28	30	10273	19830	58665	58	30	06412	23691	69403
29	00	10199	19904	58859	59	00	06357	23746	69568
29	30	10126	19977	59052	59	30	06302	23801	69733
30	00	10053	10050	59244	60	00	06247	23856	69897

M	S	Elapf. Time.	Middle Time.	Rising.	M	S	Elapf. Time.	Middle Time.	Rising.
00	30	0.06192	5.23911	4.70001	30	30	0.03399	5.26704	4.79193
01	00	06138	23965	70224	31	00	03360	26743	79334
01	30	06084	24019	70387	31	30	03321	26782	79475
02	00	06030	24073	70550	32	00	03283	26820	79616
02	30	05977	24126	70712	32	30	03245	26858	79756
03	00	05924	24179	70874	33	00	03207	26896	79896
03	30	05871	24232	71036	33	30	03170	26934	80036
04	00	05818	24285	71197	34	00	03132	26971	80175
04	30	05766	24337	71352	34	30	03095	27008	80314
05	00	05714	24389	71518	35	00	03058	27045	80452
05	30	0.05662	5.24441	4.71678	35	30	0.03021	5.27082	4.80591
06	00	05610	24493	71837	36	00	02985	27118	80729
06	30	05559	24544	71996	36	30	02949	27154	80867
07	00	05508	24595	72155	37	00	02913	27190	81004
07	30	05457	24646	72313	37	30	02877	[illegible]	81141
08	00	[illegible]	24697	72471	38	00	02841	[illegible]	[illegible]
08	30	05356	24747	72629	38	30	02806	27297	81414
09	00	05306	24797	72786	39	00	02771	[illegible]	81550
09	30	05256	24847	72942	39	30	[illegible]	[illegible]	81686
10	00	[illegible]	[illegible]	[illegible]	40	00	[illegible]	[illegible]	[illegible]
10	30	[illegible]	[illegible]	4.73254	40	30	[illegible]	[illegible]	4.81956
11	00	[illegible]	[illegible]	[illegible]	41	00	[illegible]	[illegible]	82091
11	30	[illegible]	25043	73565	41	30	[illegible]	[illegible]	82226
12	00	[illegible]	[illegible]	[illegible]	42	00	02565	[illegible]	82360
12	30	[illegible]	25139	73874	42	30	[illegible]	[illegible]	82493
13	00	04916	25187	[illegible]	43	00	[illegible]	[illegible]	[illegible]
13	30	04868	25235	[illegible]	43	30	[illegible]	[illegible]	[illegible]
14	00	04821	25282	[illegible]	44	00	[illegible]	[illegible]	[illegible]
14	30	04774	25329	74488	44	30	[illegible]	[illegible]	[illegible]
15	00	04727	25376	74641	45	00	02368	[illegible]	[illegible]
15	30	0.04680	5.25423	4.74793	45	30	0.02336	[illegible]	4.83291
16	00	04634	25469	74944	46	00	02304	27794	83423
16	30	04588	25515	75096	46	30	02272	[illegible]	83554
17	00	04542	25561	75247	47	00	02241	27862	83685
17	30	04496	25607	75398	47	30	02210	27893	83816
18	00	04451	25652	75549	48	00	02179	27924	83947
18	30	04406	25697	75699	48	30	02148	27955	84077
19	00	04361	25742	75848	49	00	02118	27985	84207
19	30	04316	25787	75997	49	30	02088	28015	84337
20	00	04272	25831	76146	50	00	02058	28045	84466
20	30	0.04228	5.25875	4.76295	50	30	0.02028	5.28075	4.84595
21	00	04184	25919	76443	51	00	01998	28105	84724
21	30	04141	25962	76591	51	30	01969	28134	84853
22	00	04098	26005	76738	52	00	01940	28163	84981
22	30	04055	26048	76885	52	30	01911	28192	85109
23	00	04012	26091	77032	53	00	01882	28221	85236
23	30	03969	26134	77179	53	30	01854	28249	85363
24	00	03927	26176	77325	54	00	01826	28277	85490
24	30	03885	26218	77471	54	30	01798	28305	85617
25	00	03843	26260	77616	55	00	01770	28333	85744
25	30	0.03801	5.26302	4.77761	55	30	0.01743	5.28360	4.85870
26	00	03760	26343	77906	56	00	01716	28387	85996
26	30	03719	26384	78050	56	30	01689	28414	86121
27	00	03678	26425	78194	57	00	01662	28441	86246
27	30	03638	26466	78338	57	30	01635	28468	86371
28	00	03597	26506	78481	58	00	01609	28494	86496
28	30	03557	26546	78624	58	30	01583	28520	86621
29	00	03517	26586	78767	59	00	01557	28546	86745
29	30	03478	26626	78909	59	30	01531	28572	86869
30	00	03438	26665	79051	60	00	[illegible]	28598	86993

M	S.	½ Elapſ. Time.	Middle Time.	Riſing.	M	S	½ Elapſ. Time.	Middle Time.	Riſing.
00	30	01480	5.28623	4.87116	30	30	0.00361	5.29742	4.94033
01	00	01455	28648	87239	31	00	00349	29754	94141
01	30	01430	28673	87362	31	30	00337	29766	94248
02	00	01405	28698	87484	32	00	00325	29778	94356
02	30	01381	28722	87606	32	30	00313	29790	94463
03	00	01357	28746	87728	33	00	00302	29801	94570
03	30	01333	28770	87850	33	30	00291	29812	94676
04	00	01309	28794	87971	34	00	00280	29823	94782
04	30	01286	28817	88092	34	30	00269	29834	94888
05	00	01263	28840	88213	35	00	00259	29844	94994
05	30	0.01240	5.28863	4.88334	35	30	0.00249	5.29854	4.95100
06	00	01217	28886	88454	36	00	00239	29864	95205
06	30	01194	28909	88574	36	30	00229	29874	95310
07	00	01172	28931	88694	37	00	00219	29884	95415
07	30	01150	28953	88814	37	30	00209	29894	95520
08	00	01128	28975	88933	38	00	00200	29903	95624
08	30	01106	28997	89052	38	30	00191	29912	95728
09	00	01084	29019	89171	39	00	00182	29921	95832
09	30	01063	29040	89289	39	30	00174	29929	95936
10	00	01042	29061	89407	40	00	00166	29937	96040
10	30	0.01021	5.29082	4.89525	40	30	0.00157	5.29945	4.96143
11	00	01000	29103	89643	41	00	00150	29953	96246
11	30	00980	29123	89760	41	30	00142	29961	96349
12	00	00960	29143	89877	42	00	00134	29969	96452
12	30	00940	29163	89994	42	30	00127	29976	96554
13	00	00920	29183	90111	43	00	00120	29983	96656
13	30	00900	29203	90227	43	30	00113	29990	96758
14	00	00881	29222	90343	44	00	00106	29997	96860
14	30	00862	29241	90459	44	30	00099	30004	96961
15	00	00843	29260	90575	45	00	00093	30010	97062
15	30	0.00824	5.29279	4.90690	45	30	0.00087	5.30016	4.97163
16	00	00805	29298	90805	46	00	00081	30022	97264
16	30	00787	29316	90920	46	30	00075	30028	97365
17	00	00769	29334	91035	47	00	00070	30033	97465
17	30	00751	29352	91149	47	30	00065	30038	97565
18	00	00733	29370	91263	48	00	00060	30043	97665
18	30	00716	29387	91377	48	30	00055	30048	97765
19	00	00699	29404	91490	49	00	00050	30053	97865
19	30	00682	29421	91603	49	30	00045	30058	97964
20	00	00665	29438	91716	50	00	00041	30062	98063
20	30	0.00648	5.29455	4.91829	50	30	0.00037	5.30066	4.98162
21	00	00632	29471	91942	51	00	00033	30070	98261
21	30	00616	29487	92054	51	30	00029	30074	98359
22	00	00600	29503	92166	52	00	00026	30077	98457
22	30	00584	29519	92278	52	30	00023	30080	98555
23	00	00568	29535	92390	53	00	00020	30083	98653
23	30	00553	29550	92501	53	30	00017	30086	98751
24	00	00538	29565	92612	54	00	00015	30088	98848
24	30	00523	29580	92723	54	30	00012	30090	98945
25	00	00508	29595	92834	55	00	00010	30092	99042
25	30	0.00494	5.29609	4.92944	55	30	0.00008	5.30094	4.99139
26	00	00480	29623	93054	56	00	00007	30096	99236
26	30	00466	29637	93164	56	30	00005	30098	99332
27	00	00452	29651	93274	57	00	00004	30099	99428
27	30	00438	29665	93383	57	30	00003	30100	99524
28	00	00425	29678	93492	58	00	00002	30101	99620
28	30	00412	29691	93601	58	30	00001	30102	99715
29	00	00399	29704	93709	59	00	00000	30103	99810
29	30	00386	29717	93817	59	30	00000	30103	99905
30	00	00373	5.29730	93925	60	0	00000	30103	5.00000

	0		1		2		3		4		
M	N.sine	N.cos	N.sine	N.cos	N.sine	N.cos	N.sine	N.cos	N.sine	N.cos	M
0	00	100000	1745	99985	3490	99939	5234	99863	6976	99756	60
1	29	0000	1774	984	3519	938	5263	861	7005	754	59
2	58	0000	1803	984	3548	937	5292	860	7034	752	58
3	87	0000	1832	983	3577	936	5321	858	7063	750	57
4	116	0000	1862	983	3606	935	5350	857	7092	748	56
5	145	0000	1891	982	3635	934	5379	855	7121	746	55
6	175	0000	1920	982	3664	933	5408	854	7150	744	54
7	204	100000	1949	99981	3693	99932	5437	99852	7179	99742	53
8	233	0000	1978	980	3723	931	5466	851	7208	740	52
9	262	0000	2007	980	3752	930	5495	849	7237	738	51
10	291	0000	2036	979	3781	929	5524	847	7266	736	50
11	323	99999	2065	979	3810	927	5553	846	7295	734	49
12	349	999	2094	978	3839	927	5582	844	7324	731	48
13	378	99999	2123	99977	3868	99925	5611	99842	7353	99729	47
14	407	999	2152	977	3897	924	5640	841	7382	727	46
15	436	999	2181	976	3926	923	5669	839	7411	725	45
16	465	999	2211	976	3955	922	5698	838	7440	723	44
17	495	999	2240	975	3984	921	5727	836	7469	721	43
18	524	999	2269	974	4013	919	5756	834	7498	719	42
19	553	99998	2298	99974	4042	99918	5785	99833	7527	99716	41
20	582	998	2327	973	4071	917	5814	831	7556	714	40
21	611	998	2356	972	4100	916	5844	829	7585	712	39
22	640	998	2385	972	4129	915	5873	827	7614	710	38
23	669	998	2414	971	4159	914	5902	826	7643	708	37
24	698	998	2443	970	4188	912	5931	824	7672	705	36
25	727	99997	2472	99969	4217	99911	5960	99822	7701	99703	35
26	756	997	2501	969	4246	910	5989	821	7730	701	34
27	785	997	2530	968	4275	909	6018	819	7759	699	33
28	814	997	2560	967	4304	907	6047	817	7788	696	32
29	844	996	2589	966	4333	906	6076	815	7817	694	31
30	873	996	2618	966	4362	905	6105	813	7846	692	30
31	902	99996	2647	99965	4391	99904	6134	99812	7875	99689	29
32	931	996	2676	964	4420	902	6163	810	7904	687	28
33	960	995	2705	963	4449	901	6192	808	7933	685	27
34	989	995	2734	963	4478	900	6221	806	7962	683	26
35	1018	995	2763	962	4507	898	6250	804	7991	680	25
36	1047	995	2792	961	4536	897	6279	803	8020	678	24
37	1076	99994	2821	99960	4565	99896	6308	99801	8049	99676	23
38	1105	994	2850	959	4594	894	6337	799	8078	673	22
39	1134	994	2879	959	4623	893	6366	797	8107	671	21
40	1164	993	2908	958	4653	892	6395	795	8136	668	20
41	1193	993	2938	957	4682	890	6424	793	8165	666	19
42	1222	993	2967	956	4711	889	6453	792	8194	664	18
43	1251	99992	2996	99955	4740	99888	6482	99790	8223	99661	17
44	1280	992	3025	954	4769	886	6511	788	8252	659	16
45	1309	991	3054	953	4798	885	6540	786	8281	657	15
46	1338	991	3083	952	4827	883	6569	784	8310	654	14
47	1367	991	3112	952	4856	882	6598	782	8339	652	13
48	1396	990	3141	951	4885	881	6627	780	8368	649	12
49	1425	99990	3170	99950	4914	99879	6656	99778	8397	99647	11
50	1454	989	3199	949	4943	878	6685	776	8426	644	10
51	1483	989	3228	948	4972	876	6714	774	8455	642	9
52	1513	989	3257	947	5001	875	6743	772	8484	639	8
53	1542	988	3286	946	5030	873	6773	770	8513	637	7
54	1571	988	3316	945	5059	872	6802	768	8542	635	6
55	1600	99987	3345	99944	5088	99870	6831	99766	8571	99632	5
56	1629	987	3374	943	5117	869	6860	764	8600	630	4
57	1658	986	3403	942	5146	867	6889	762	8629	627	3
58	1687	986	3432	941	5175	866	6918	760	8658	625	2
59	1716	985	3461	940	5205	864	6947	758	8687	622	1
	N.cos	N.sine	N.cos	N.sine	N.cos	N.sine	N.cos	N.sine	N.cos	N.sine	
	89		88		87		86		85		

	5		6		7		8		9		
M	N.sine	N.cos	N.sine	N.cos	N.sine	N.cos	N.sine	N.cos	N.sine	N.cos	M
0	8716	99619	10453	99452	12187	99255	13917	99027	15643	98769	60
1	8745	617	482	449	216	251	946	023	672	764	59
2	8774	614	511	446	245	248	975	019	701	760	58
3	8803	612	540	443	274	244	14004	015	730	755	57
4	8831	609	569	440	302	240	033	011	758	751	56
5	8860	607	597	437	331	237	061	006	787	746	55
6	8889	604	626	434	360	233	090	002	816	741	54
7	8918	99602	10655	99431	12389	99230	14119	98998	15845	98737	53
8	8947	599	684	428	418	226	148	994	873	732	52
9	8976	596	713	424	447	222	177	990	902	728	51
10	9005	594	742	421	476	219	205	986	931	723	50
11	9034	591	771	418	504	215	234	982	959	718	49
12	9063	588	800	415	533	211	263	978	988	714	48
13	9092	99586	10829	99412	12562	99208	14292	98973	16017	98709	47
14	9121	583	858	409	591	204	320	969	046	704	46
15	9150	580	887	406	620	200	349	965	074	700	45
16	9179	578	916	402	649	197	378	961	103	695	44
17	9208	575	945	399	678	193	407	957	132	690	43
18	9237	572	973	396	706	189	436	953	160	686	42
19	9266	99570	11002	99393	12735	99186	14464	98948	16189	98681	41
20	9295	567	031	390	764	182	493	944	218	676	40
21	9324	564	060	386	793	178	522	940	246	671	39
22	9353	562	089	383	822	175	551	936	275	667	38
23	9382	559	118	380	851	171	580	931	304	662	37
24	9411	556	147	377	880	167	608	927	333	657	36
25	9440	99553	11176	99374	12908	99163	14637	98923	16361	98652	35
26	9469	551	205	370	937	160	666	919	390	648	34
27	9498	548	234	367	966	156	695	914	419	643	33
28	9527	545	263	364	995	152	723	910	447	638	32
29	9556	542	292	360	13024	148	752	906	476	633	31
30	9585	540	320	357	053	144	781	902	505	629	30
31	9614	99537	11349	99354	13081	99141	14810	98897	16533	98624	29
32	9642	534	378	351	110	137	838	893	562	619	28
33	9671	531	407	347	139	133	867	889	591	614	27
34	9700	528	436	344	168	129	896	884	620	609	26
35	9729	526	465	341	197	125	925	880	648	604	25
36	9758	523	494	337	226	122	954	876	677	600	24
37	9787	99520	11523	99334	13254	99118	14982	98871	16706	98595	23
38	9816	517	552	331	283	114	15011	867	734	590	22
39	9845	514	580	327	312	110	040	863	763	585	21
40	9874	511	609	324	341	106	069	858	792	580	20
41	9903	508	638	320	370	102	097	854	820	575	19
42	9932	506	667	317	399	098	126	849	849	570	18
43	9961	99503	11696	99314	13427	99094	15155	98845	16878	98565	17
44	9990	500	725	310	456	091	184	841	906	561	16
45	10019	497	754	307	485	087	212	836	935	556	15
46	10048	494	783	303	514	083	241	832	964	551	14
47	10077	491	812	300	543	079	270	827	992	546	13
48	10106	488	840	297	572	075	299	823	17021	541	12
49	10135	99485	11869	99293	13600	99071	15327	98818	17050	98536	11
50	10164	482	898	290	629	067	356	814	078	531	10
51	10192	479	927	286	658	063	385	809	107	526	9
52	10221	476	956	283	687	059	414	805	136	521	8
53	10250	473	985	279	716	055	442	800	164	516	7
54	10279	470	12014	276	744	051	471	796	193	511	6
55	10308	99467	12043	99272	13773	99047	15500	98791	17222	98506	5
56	10337	464	071	269	802	043	529	787	250	501	4
57	10366	461	100	265	831	039	557	782	279	496	3
58	10395	458	129	262	860	035	586	778	308	491	2
59	10424	455	158	258	889	031	615	773	336	486	1
	N.cos	N.sine	N.cos	N.sine	N.cos	N.sine	N.cos	N.sine	N.cos	N.sine	
	84		83		82		81		80		

	10		11		12		13		14		
M	N.sine	N.cos	N.sine	N.cos	N.sine	N.cos	N.sine	N.cos	N.sine	N.cos	M
0	17365	98481	19081	98163	20791	97815	22495	97437	24192	97030	60
1	393	476	109	157	820	809	523	430	220	023	59
2	422	471	138	152	848	803	552	424	249	015	58
3	451	466	167	146	877	797	580	417	277	008	57
4	479	460	195	140	905	790	608	411	305	001	56
5	508	455	224	135	933	784	637	404	333	96994	55
6	537	450	252	129	962	778	665	398	361	987	54
7	17565	98445	19281	98124	20990	97772	22693	97391	24390	96980	53
8	594	440	309	118	21019	766	722	384	418	973	52
9	623	435	338	112	047	760	750	378	446	966	51
10	651	430	366	107	076	754	778	371	474	959	50
11	680	425	395	101	104	748	807	365	503	952	49
12	708	420	423	096	132	742	835	358	531	945	48
13	17737	98414	19452	98090	21161	97735	22863	97351	24559	96937	47
14	766	409	480	084	189	729	892	345	587	930	46
15	794	404	509	079	218	723	920	338	615	923	45
16	823	399	538	073	246	717	948	331	644	916	44
17	852	394	566	067	275	711	977	325	672	909	43
18	880	388	595	061	303	705	23005	318	700	902	42
19	17909	98383	19623	98056	21331	97698	23033	97311	24728	96894	41
20	937	378	652	050	360	692	062	304	756	887	40
21	966	373	680	044	388	686	090	298	784	880	39
22	995	368	709	039	417	680	118	291	813	873	38
23	18023	362	737	033	445	673	146	284	841	866	37
24	052	357	766	027	474	667	175	278	869	858	36
25	18081	98352	19794	98021	21502	97661	23203	97271	24897	96851	35
26	109	347	823	016	530	655	231	264	925	844	34
27	138	341	851	010	559	648	260	257	953	837	33
28	166	336	880	004	587	642	288	251	982	829	32
29	195	331	908	97998	616	636	316	244	25010	822	31
30	224	325	937	992	644	630	345	237	038	815	30
31	18252	98320	19965	97987	21672	97623	23373	97230	25066	96807	29
32	281	315	994	981	701	617	401	223	094	800	28
33	309	310	20022	975	729	611	429	217	122	793	27
34	338	304	051	969	758	604	458	210	151	786	26
35	367	299	079	963	786	598	486	203	179	778	25
36	395	294	108	958	814	592	514	196	207	771	24
37	18424	98288	20136	97952	21843	97585	23542	97189	25235	96764	23
38	452	283	165	946	871	579	571	182	263	756	22
39	481	277	193	940	899	573	599	176	291	749	21
40	509	272	222	934	928	566	627	169	320	742	20
41	538	267	250	928	956	560	656	162	348	734	19
42	567	261	279	922	985	553	684	155	376	727	18
43	18595	98256	20307	97916	22013	97547	23712	97148	25404	96719	17
44	624	250	336	910	041	541	740	141	432	712	16
45	652	245	364	905	070	534	769	134	460	705	15
46	681	240	393	899	098	528	797	127	488	697	14
47	710	234	421	893	126	521	825	120	516	690	13
48	738	229	450	887	155	515	853	113	545	682	12
49	18767	98223	20478	97881	22183	97508	23882	97106	25573	96675	11
50	795	218	507	875	212	502	910	100	601	667	10
51	824	212	535	869	240	496	938	093	629	660	9
52	852	207	563	863	268	489	966	086	657	653	8
53	881	201	592	857	297	483	995	079	685	645	7
54	910	196	620	851	325	476	24023	072	713	638	6
55	18938	98190	20649	97845	22353	97470	24051	97065	25741	96630	5
56	967	185	677	839	382	463	079	058	769	623	4
57	995	179	706	833	410	457	108	051	798	615	3
58	19024	174	734	827	438	450	136	044	826	608	2
59	052	168	763	821	467	444	164	037	854	600	1
	N.cos	N.sine	N.cos	N.sine	N.cos	N.sine	N.cos	N.sine	N.cos	N.sine	
	79		78		77		76		75		

	15		16		17		18		19		
M	N.sine	N.cos	N.sine	N.cos	N.sine	N.cos	N.sine	N.cos	N.sine	N.cos	M
0	25882	96593	27564	96126	29237	95630	30902	95106	32557	94552	60
1	910	585	592	118	265	622	929	097	584	542	59
2	938	578	620	110	293	613	957	088	612	533	58
3	966	570	648	102	321	605	985	079	639	523	57
4	994	562	676	094	348	596	31012	070	667	514	56
5	26022	555	704	086	376	588	040	061	694	504	55
6	050	547	731	078	404	579	068	052	722	495	54
7	26079	96540	27759	96070	29432	95571	31095	95043	32749	94485	53
8	107	532	787	062	460	562	123	033	777	476	52
9	135	524	815	054	487	554	151	024	804	466	51
10	163	517	843	046	515	545	178	015	832	457	50
11	191	509	871	037	543	536	206	006	859	447	49
12	219	502	899	029	571	528	233	94997	887	438	48
13	26247	96494	27927	96021	29599	95519	31261	94988	32914	94428	47
14	275	486	955	013	626	511	289	979	942	418	46
15	303	479	983	005	654	502	316	970	969	409	45
16	331	471	28011	95997	682	493	344	961	997	399	44
17	359	463	039	989	710	485	372	952	33024	390	43
18	387	456	067	981	737	476	399	943	051	380	42
19	26415	96448	28095	95972	29765	95467	31427	94933	33079	94370	41
20	443	440	123	964	793	459	454	923	106	361	40
21	471	433	150	956	821	450	482	915	134	351	39
22	500	425	178	948	849	441	510	906	161	342	38
23	528	417	206	940	876	433	537	897	189	332	37
24	556	410	234	931	904	424	565	888	216	322	36
25	26584	96402	28262	95923	29932	95415	31592	94878	33244	94313	35
26	612	394	290	915	960	407	620	869	271	303	34
27	640	386	318	907	987	398	648	860	298	293	33
28	668	379	346	898	30015	389	675	851	326	284	32
29	696	371	374	890	043	380	703	842	353	274	31
30	724	363	402	882	071	372	730	832	381	264	30
31	26752	96355	28429	95874	30098	95363	31758	94823	33408	94254	29
32	780	347	457	865	126	354	786	814	436	245	28
33	808	340	485	857	154	345	813	805	463	235	27
34	836	332	513	849	182	337	841	795	490	225	26
35	864	324	541	841	209	328	868	786	518	216	25
36	892	316	569	832	237	319	896	777	545	206	24
37	26920	96308	28597	95824	30265	95310	31923	94768	33573	94196	23
38	948	301	625	816	292	301	951	758	600	186	22
39	976	293	652	807	320	293	979	749	627	176	21
40	27004	285	680	799	348	284	32006	740	655	167	20
41	032	277	708	791	376	275	034	730	682	157	19
42	060	269	736	782	403	266	061	721	710	147	18
43	27088	96261	28764	95774	30431	95257	32089	94712	33737	94137	17
44	116	253	792	766	459	248	116	702	764	127	16
45	144	246	820	757	486	240	144	693	792	118	15
46	172	238	847	749	514	231	171	684	819	108	14
47	200	230	875	740	542	222	199	674	846	098	13
48	228	222	903	732	570	213	227	665	874	088	12
49	27256	96214	28931	95724	30597	95204	32254	94656	33901	94078	11
50	284	206	959	715	625	195	282	646	929	068	10
51	312	198	987	707	653	186	309	637	956	058	9
52	340	190	29015	698	680	177	337	627	983	049	8
53	368	182	042	690	708	168	364	618	34011	039	7
54	396	174	070	681	736	159	392	609	038	029	6
55	27424	96166	29098	95673	30763	95150	32419	94599	34065	94019	5
56	452	158	126	664	791	142	447	590	093	009	4
57	480	150	154	656	819	133	474	580	120	93999	3
58	508	142	182	647	846	124	502	571	147	989	2
60	536	134	209	639	874	115	529	561	175	979	1
	N.cos	N.sine	N.cos	N.sine	N.cos	N.sine	N.cos	N.sine	N.cos	N.sine	
	74		73		72		71		70		

	20		21		22		23		24		
M	N.ſine	N.coſ	N.ſine	N.coſ	N.ſine	N.coſ	N.ſine	N.coſ	N.ſine	N.coſ	M
0	34202	93969	35837	93358	37461	92718	39073	92050	40674	91355	60
1	229	959	864	348	488	707	100	039	700	343	59
2	257	949	891	337	515	697	127	028	727	331	58
3	284	939	918	327	542	686	153	016	753	319	57
4	311	929	945	316	569	675	180	005	780	307	56
5	339	919	973	306	595	664	207	91994	806	295	55
6	366	909	36000	295	622	653	234	982	833	283	54
7	34393	93899	36027	93285	37649	92642	39260	91971	40860	91272	53
8	421	889	054	274	676	631	287	959	886	260	52
9	448	879	081	264	703	620	314	948	913	248	51
10	475	869	108	253	730	609	341	936	939	236	50
11	503	859	135	243	757	598	367	925	966	224	49
12	530	849	162	232	784	587	394	914	992	212	48
13	34557	93839	36190	93222	37811	92576	39421	91902	41019	91200	47
14	584	829	217	211	838	565	448	891	045	188	46
15	612	819	244	201	865	554	474	879	072	176	45
16	639	809	271	190	892	543	501	868	098	164	44
17	666	799	298	180	919	532	528	856	125	152	43
18	694	789	325	169	946	521	555	845	151	140	42
19	34721	93779	36352	93159	37973	92510	39581	91833	41178	91128	41
20	748	769	379	148	999	499	608	822	204	116	40
21	775	759	406	137	38026	488	635	810	231	104	39
22	803	748	433	127	053	477	661	799	257	092	38
23	830	738	461	116	080	466	688	787	284	080	37
24	857	728	488	106	107	455	715	775	310	068	36
25	34884	93718	36515	93095	38134	92444	39741	91764	41337	91056	35
26	912	708	542	084	161	432	768	752	363	044	34
27	939	698	569	074	188	421	795	741	390	032	33
28	966	688	596	063	215	410	822	729	416	020	32
29	993	677	623	052	241	399	848	718	443	008	31
30	35021	667	650	042	268	388	875	706	469	90996	30
31	35048	93657	36677	93031	38295	92377	39902	91694	41496	90984	29
32	075	647	704	020	322	366	928	683	522	972	28
33	102	637	731	010	349	355	955	671	549	960	27
34	130	626	758	92999	376	343	982	660	575	948	26
35	157	616	785	988	403	332	40008	648	602	936	25
36	184	606	812	978	430	321	035	636	628	924	24
37	35211	93596	36839	92967	38456	92310	40062	91625	41655	90911	23
38	239	585	867	956	483	299	088	613	681	899	22
39	266	575	894	945	510	287	115	601	707	887	21
40	293	565	921	935	537	276	141	590	734	875	20
41	320	555	948	924	564	265	168	578	760	863	19
42	347	544	975	913	591	254	195	566	787	851	18
43	35375	93534	37002	92902	38617	92243	40221	91555	41813	90839	17
44	402	524	029	892	644	231	248	543	840	826	16
45	429	514	056	881	671	220	275	531	866	814	15
46	456	503	083	870	698	209	301	519	892	802	14
47	483	493	110	859	725	198	328	508	919	790	13
48	511	483	137	849	752	186	355	496	945	778	12
49	35538	93472	37164	92838	38778	92175	40381	91484	41972	90766	11
50	565	462	191	827	805	164	408	472	998	753	10
51	592	452	218	816	832	152	434	461	42024	741	9
52	619	441	245	805	859	141	461	449	051	729	8
53	647	431	272	794	886	130	488	437	077	717	7
54	674	420	299	784	912	119	514	425	104	704	6
55	35701	93410	37326	92773	38939	92107	40541	91414	42130	90692	5
56	728	400	353	762	966	096	567	402	156	680	4
57	755	389	380	751	993	085	594	390	183	668	3
58	782	379	407	740	39020	073	621	378	209	655	2
59	810	368	434	729	046	062	647	366	235	643	1
	N.coſ	N.ſine	N.coſ	N.ſine	N.coſ	N.ſine	N.coſ	N.ſine	N.coſ	N.ſine	
	69		68		67		66		65		

	25		26		27		28		29		
M	N.sine	N.cos	N.sine	N.cos	N.sine	N.cos	N.sine	N.cos	N.sine	N.cos	M
0	42262	90631	43837	89879	45399	89101	46947	88295	48481	87462	60
1	288	618	863	867	425	087	973	281	506	448	59
2	315	606	889	854	451	074	999	267	532	434	58
3	341	594	916	841	477	061	47024	254	557	420	57
4	367	582	942	828	503	048	050	240	583	406	56
5	394	569	968	816	529	035	076	226	608	391	55
6	420	557	994	803	554	021	101	213	634	377	54
7	42446	90545	44020	89790	45580	89008	47127	88199	48659	87363	53
8	473	532	046	777	606	995	153	185	684	349	52
9	499	520	072	764	632	981	178	172	710	335	51
10	525	507	098	752	658	968	204	158	735	321	50
11	552	495	124	739	684	955	229	144	761	306	49
12	578	483	151	726	710	942	255	130	786	292	48
13	42604	90470	44177	89713	45736	88928	47281	88117	48811	87278	47
14	631	458	203	700	762	915	306	103	837	264	46
15	657	446	229	687	787	902	332	089	862	250	45
16	683	433	255	674	813	88888	358	075	888	235	44
17	709	421	281	662	839	875	383	062	913	221	43
18	736	408	307	649	865	862	409	048	938	207	42
19	42762	90396	44333	89636	45891	88848	47434	88034	48964	87193	41
20	788	383	359	623	917	835	460	020	989	178	40
21	815	371	385	610	942	822	486	006	49014	164	39
22	841	358	411	597	968	808	511	87993	040	150	38
23	867	346	437	584	994	795	537	979	065	136	37
24	894	334	464	571	46020	782	562	965	090	121	36
25	42920	90321	44490	89558	46046	88768	47588	87951	49116	87107	35
26	946	309	516	545	072	755	614	937	141	093	34
27	972	296	542	532	097	741	639	923	166	079	33
28	43099	284	568	519	123	728	665	909	192	064	32
29	025	271	594	506	149	715	690	896	217	050	31
30	051	259	620	493	175	701	716	882	242	036	30
31	43077	90246	44646	89480	46201	88688	47741	87868	49268	87021	29
32	104	233	672	467	226	674	767	854	293	007	28
33	130	221	698	454	252	661	793	840	318	86993	27
34	156	208	724	441	278	647	818	826	344	978	26
35	182	196	750	428	304	634	844	812	369	964	25
36	209	183	776	415	330	620	869	798	394	949	24
37	43235	90171	44802	89402	46355	88607	47895	87784	49419	86935	23
38	261	158	828	389	381	593	920	770	445	921	22
39	287	146	854	376	407	580	946	756	470	906	21
40	313	133	880	363	433	566	972	743	495	892	20
41	340	120	906	350	458	553	997	729	521	878	19
42	366	108	932	337	484	539	48022	715	546	863	18
43	43392	90095	44958	89324	46510	88526	48048	87701	49571	86849	17
44	418	082	984	311	536	512	073	687	596	834	16
45	445	070	45010	298	561	499	099	673	622	820	15
46	471	057	036	285	587	485	124	659	647	805	14
47	497	045	062	272	613	472	150	645	672	791	13
48	523	032	088	259	639	458	175	631	695	777	12
49	43549	90019	45114	89245	46664	88445	48201	87617	49723	86762	11
50	575	007	140	232	690	431	226	603	748	748	10
51	602	89994	166	219	716	417	252	589	773	733	9
52	628	981	192	206	742	404	277	575	798	719	8
53	654	968	218	193	767	390	303	560	824	704	7
54	680	956	243	180	793	377	328	546	849	690	6
55	43706	89943	45269	89167	46819	88363	48354	87532	49874	86675	5
56	732	930	295	153	844	349	379	518	899	661	4
57	759	918	321	140	870	336	405	504	924	646	3
58	785	905	347	127	896	322	430	490	950	632	2
59	811	892	373	114	921	308	456	476	975	617	1
	N.cos	N.sine	N.cos	N.sine	N.cos	N.sine	N.cos	N.sine	N.cos	N.sine	
	64		63		62		61		60		

	30		31		32		33		34		
M	N.sine	N.cos	N.sine	N.cos	N.sine	N.cos	N.sine	N.cos	N.sine	N.cos	M
0	50000	86603	51504	85717	52992	84805	54464	83867	55919	82904	60
1	025	588	529	702	53017	789	488	851	943	887	59
2	050	573	554	687	041	774	513	835	968	871	58
3	076	559	579	672	066	759	537	819	992	855	57
4	101	544	604	657	091	743	561	804	56016	839	56
5	126	530	628	642	115	728	586	788	040	822	55
6	151	515	653	627	140	712	610	772	064	806	54
7	50176	86501	51678	85612	53164	84697	54635	83756	56088	82790	53
8	201	486	703	597	189	681	659	740	112	773	52
9	227	471	728	582	214	666	683	724	136	757	51
10	252	457	753	567	238	650	708	708	160	741	50
11	277	442	778	551	263	635	732	692	184	724	49
12	302	427	803	536	288	619	756	676	208	708	48
13	50327	86413	51828	85521	53312	84604	54781	83660	56232	82692	47
14	352	398	852	506	337	588	805	645	256	675	46
15	377	384	877	491	361	573	829	629	280	659	45
16	403	369	902	476	386	557	854	613	305	643	44
17	428	354	927	461	411	542	878	597	329	626	43
18	453	340	952	446	435	526	902	581	353	610	42
19	50478	86325	51977	85431	53460	84511	54927	83565	56377	82593	41
20	503	310	52002	416	484	495	951	549	401	577	40
21	528	295	026	401	509	480	975	533	425	561	39
22	553	281	051	385	534	464	999	517	449	544	38
23	578	266	076	370	558	448	55024	501	473	528	37
24	603	251	101	355	583	433	048	485	497	511	36
25	50628	86237	52126	85340	53607	84417	55072	83469	56521	82495	35
26	654	222	151	325	632	402	097	453	545	478	34
27	679	207	175	310	656	386	121	437	569	462	33
28	704	192	200	294	681	370	145	421	593	446	32
29	729	178	225	279	705	355	169	405	617	429	31
30	754	163	250	264	730	339	194	389	641	413	30
31	50779	86148	52275	85249	53754	84324	55218	83373	56665	82396	29
32	804	133	299	234	779	308	242	356	689	380	28
33	829	119	324	218	804	292	266	340	713	363	27
34	854	104	349	203	828	277	291	324	736	347	26
35	879	089	374	188	853	261	315	308	760	330	25
36	904	074	398	173	877	245	339	292	784	314	24
37	50929	86059	52423	85157	53902	84230	55363	83276	56808	82297	23
38	954	045	448	142	926	214	388	260	832	281	22
39	979	030	473	127	951	198	412	244	856	264	21
40	51004	015	498	112	975	182	436	228	880	248	20
41	029	000	522	096	54000	167	460	212	904	231	19
42	054	85985	547	081	024	151	484	195	928	214	18
43	51079	85970	52572	85066	54049	84135	55509	83179	56952	82198	17
44	104	956	597	051	073	120	533	163	976	181	16
45	129	941	621	035	097	104	557	147	57000	165	15
46	154	926	646	020	122	088	581	131	024	148	14
47	179	911	671	005	146	073	605	115	047	132	13
48	204	896	696	84989	171	057	630	098	071	115	12
49	51229	85881	52720	84974	54195	84041	55654	83082	57095	82098	11
50	254	866	745	959	220	025	678	066	119	082	10
51	279	851	770	943	244	009	702	050	143	065	9
52	304	836	794	928	269	83994	726	034	167	048	8
53	329	821	819	913	293	978	750	017	191	032	7
54	354	806	844	897	317	962	775	001	215	015	6
55	51379	85792	52869	84882	54342	83946	55799	82985	57238	81999	5
56	404	777	893	866	366	930	823	969	262	982	4
57	429	762	918	851	391	915	847	953	286	965	3
58	454	747	943	836	415	899	871	936	310	949	2
59	479	732	967	820	440	883	895	920	334	932	1
	N.cos	N.sine	N.cos	N.sine	N.cos	N.sine	N.cos	N.sine	N.cos	N.sine	
	59		58		57		56		55		

	35		36		37		38		39		
M	N.sine	N.cos	N.sine	N.cos	N.sine	N.cos	N.sine	N.cos	N.sine	N.cos	M
0	57358	81915	58779	80902	60181	79864	61566	78801	62932	77715	60
1	381	899	802	885	205	846	589	783	955	696	59
2	405	882	826	867	228	829	612	765	977	678	58
3	429	865	849	850	251	811	635	747	63000	660	57
4	453	848	873	833	274	793	658	729	022	641	56
5	477	832	896	816	298	776	681	711	045	623	55
6	501	815	920	799	321	758	704	693	068	605	54
7	57524	81798	58943	80782	60344	79741	61726	78676	63090	77586	53
8	548	782	967	765	367	723	749	658	113	568	52
9	572	765	990	748	390	706	772	640	135	550	51
10	596	748	59014	730	414	688	795	622	158	531	50
11	619	731	037	713	437	671	818	604	180	513	49
12	643	714	061	696	460	653	841	586	203	494	48
13	57667	81698	59084	80679	60483	79635	61864	78568	63225	77476	47
14	691	681	107	662	506	618	887	550	248	458	46
15	715	664	131	644	529	600	909	532	271	439	45
16	738	647	154	627	553	583	932	514	293	421	44
17	762	631	178	610	576	565	955	496	316	402	43
18	786	614	201	593	599	547	978	478	338	384	42
19	57809	81597	59225	80576	60622	79530	62001	78460	63361	77366	41
20	833	580	248	558	645	512	024	442	383	347	40
21	857	563	272	541	668	494	046	424	406	329	39
22	881	546	295	524	691	477	069	405	428	310	38
23	904	530	318	507	714	459	092	387	451	292	37
24	928	513	342	489	738	441	115	369	473	273	36
25	57952	81496	59365	80472	60761	79424	62138	78351	63496	77255	35
26	976	479	389	455	784	406	160	333	518	236	34
27	999	462	412	438	807	388	183	315	540	218	33
28	58023	445	435	420	830	371	206	297	563	199	32
29	047	428	459	403	853	353	229	279	585	181	31
30	070	412	482	386	876	335	251	261	608	162	30
31	58094	81395	59506	80368	60899	79318	62274	78243	63630	77144	29
32	118	378	529	351	922	300	297	225	653	125	28
33	141	361	552	334	945	282	320	206	675	107	27
34	165	344	576	316	968	264	342	188	698	088	26
35	189	327	599	299	991	247	365	170	720	070	25
36	212	310	622	282	61015	229	388	152	742	051	24
37	58236	81293	59646	80264	61038	79211	62411	78134	63765	77033	23
38	260	276	669	247	061	193	433	116	787	014	22
39	283	259	693	230	084	176	456	098	810	76996	21
40	307	242	716	212	107	158	479	079	832	977	20
41	330	225	739	195	130	140	502	061	854	959	19
42	354	208	763	178	153	122	524	043	877	940	18
43	58378	81191	59786	80160	61176	79105	62547	78025	63899	76921	17
44	401	174	809	143	199	087	570	007	922	903	16
45	425	157	832	125	222	069	592	77988	944	884	15
46	449	140	856	108	245	051	615	970	966	866	14
47	472	123	879	091	268	033	638	952	989	847	13
48	496	106	902	073	291	015	660	934	64011	828	12
49	58519	81089	59926	80056	61314	78998	62683	77916	64033	76810	11
50	543	072	949	038	337	980	706	897	056	791	10
51	567	055	972	021	360	962	728	879	078	772	9
52	590	038	995	003	383	944	751	861	100	754	8
53	614	021	60019	79986	406	926	774	843	123	735	7
54	637	004	042	968	429	908	796	824	145	717	6
55	58661	80987	60065	79951	61451	78891	62819	77806	64167	76698	5
56	684	970	089	934	474	873	842	788	190	679	4
57	708	953	112	916	497	855	864	769	212	661	3
58	731	936	135	899	520	837	887	751	234	642	2
59	755	919	158	881	543	819	909	733	256	623	1
	N.cos	N.sine	N.cos	N.sine	N.cos	N.sine	N.cos	N.sine	N.cos	N.sine	
	54		53		52		51		50		

	40		41		42		43		44		
M	N.sine	N.cos	N.sine	N.cos	N.sine	N.cos	N.sine	N.cos	N.sine	N.cos	M
0	64279	76604	65606	75471	66913	74314	68200	73135	69466	71934	60
1	301	586	628	452	935	295	221	116	487	914	59
2	323	567	650	433	956	276	242	096	508	894	58
3	346	548	672	414	978	256	264	076	529	873	57
4	368	530	694	395	999	237	285	056	549	853	56
5	390	511	716	375	67021	217	306	036	570	833	55
6	412	492	738	356	043	198	327	016	591	813	54
7	64435	76473	65759	75337	67064	74178	68349	72996	69612	71792	53
8	457	455	781	318	086	159	370	976	633	772	52
9	479	436	803	299	107	139	391	957	654	752	51
10	501	417	825	280	129	120	412	937	675	732	50
11	524	398	847	261	151	100	433	917	696	711	49
12	546	380	869	241	172	080	455	897	717	691	48
13	64568	76361	65891	75222	67194	74061	68476	72877	69737	71671	47
14	590	342	913	203	215	041	497	857	758	650	46
15	612	323	935	184	237	022	518	837	779	630	45
16	635	304	956	165	258	002	539	817	800	610	44
17	657	286	978	146	280	73983	561	797	821	590	43
18	679	267	66000	126	301	963	582	777	842	569	42
19	64701	76248	66022	75107	67323	73944	68603	72757	69862	71549	41
20	723	229	044	088	344	924	624	737	883	529	40
21	746	210	066	069	366	904	645	717	904	508	39
22	768	192	088	050	387	885	666	697	925	488	38
23	790	173	109	030	409	865	688	677	946	468	37
24	812	154	131	011	430	846	709	657	966	447	36
25	64834	76135	66153	74992	67452	73826	68730	72637	69987	71427	35
26	856	116	175	973	473	806	751	617	70008	407	34
27	878	097	197	953	495	787	772	597	029	386	33
28	901	078	218	934	516	767	793	577	049	366	32
29	923	059	240	915	538	747	814	557	070	345	31
30	945	041	262	896	559	728	835	537	091	325	30
31	64967	76022	66284	74876	67580	73708	68857	72517	70112	71305	29
32	989	003	306	857	602	688	878	497	132	284	28
33	65011	75984	327	838	623	669	899	477	153	264	27
34	033	965	349	818	645	649	920	457	174	243	26
35	055	946	371	799	666	629	941	437	195	223	25
36	077	927	393	780	688	610	962	417	215	203	24
37	65099	75908	66414	74760	67709	73590	68983	72397	70236	71182	23
38	122	889	436	741	730	570	69004	377	257	162	22
39	144	870	458	722	752	551	025	357	277	141	21
40	166	851	480	703	773	531	046	337	298	121	20
41	188	832	501	683	795	511	067	317	319	100	19
42	210	813	523	664	816	491	088	297	339	080	18
43	65232	75794	66545	74644	67837	73472	69109	72277	70360	71059	17
44	254	775	566	625	859	452	130	257	381	039	16
45	276	756	588	606	880	432	151	236	401	019	15
46	298	738	610	586	901	412	172	216	422	70998	14
47	320	719	632	567	923	393	193	196	443	978	13
48	342	699	653	548	944	373	214	176	463	957	12
49	65304	75680	66675	74528	67965	73353	69235	72156	70484	70937	11
50	386	661	697	509	987	333	256	136	505	916	10
51	408	642	718	489	68008	314	277	116	525	896	9
52	430	623	740	470	029	294	298	095	546	875	8
53	452	604	762	451	051	274	319	075	567	855	7
54	474	585	783	431	072	254	340	055	587	834	6
55	65496	75566	66805	74412	68093	73234	69361	72035	70608	70813	5
56	518	547	827	392	115	215	382	015	628	793	4
57	540	528	848	373	136	195	403	995	649	772	3
58	562	509	870	353	157	175	424	974	670	752	2
59	583	490	891	334	179	155	445	954	690	731	1
	N.cos	N.sine	N.cos	N.sine	N.cos	N.sine	N.cos	N.sine	N.cos	N.sine	
	49		48		47		46		45		

A Table of the Right Aſcenſion and Declination of ſome of the principal fixed Stars, adapted to the Year 1775, with their Annual Variation.

Names of the Stars.	Magnit.	Right aſc. in Time H.	M.	S.	Yearly Variati. S. T.	Declination. D.	M.	S.	Yearly Variati. T. S.
Pegaſus	2	0	1	41	3, 08	13	55	57N.	20 add
Eridani	1	1	29	11	2, 26	58	23	34S.	18 ſub
Arietis	2	1	54	27	3, 20	22	23	18N.	18 add
Ceti	2	2	50	34	3, 8	3	11	29N.	15 add
Aldebaran	1	4	23	7	3, 43	16	2	23N.	8 add
Capella	1	5	0	6	4, 4	45	44	50N.	5 add
Regel	1	5	3	30	3, 0	8	28	43S.	5 ſub
Taurus	2	5	12	3	3, 8	28	23	52N.	4 add
Orion	1	5	43	0	3, 3	7	20	49N.	2 add
Canobus	1	6	18	57	1, 3	52	34	47S.	1 add
Cyrius	1	6	35	12	2, 40	16	24	52S.	3 add
Caſtor	2	7	19	14	4, 0	32	21	40N.	7 ſub
Procyon	1	7	26	33	3, 12	5	47	36N.	7 ſub
Pollux	2	7	31	10	3, 75	28	33	10N.	8 ſub
Argo	1	9	8	4	0, 44	68	46	1S.	12 add
Cor. Hydra	2	9	16	32	2, 56	7	41	30S.	15 add
Regulus	1	9	56	3	3, 24	13	3	32N.	17 ſub
Urſa Major	2	10	49	16	3, 89	62	57	38N.	19 ſub
Croſiers	1	12	14	17	3, 22	61	51	7S.	20 add
Spica Virginis	1	13	13	21	3, 15	9	58	47S.	19 add
Arcturus	1	14	5	10	2, 82	10	22	31N.	17 ſu
Centaurus	1	14	24	40	4, 41	59	53	55S.	16 ad
Coronae	2	15	24	46	2, 0	27	29	5N.	12 ſub
Antares	1	16	15	36	3, 66	25	54	51S.	9 add
Sagittarius	2	18	8	11	4, 0	34	28	0S.	1 ſub
Lyra	1	18	29	7	2, c	38	34	51N.	2 add
Aquila	1	19	39	44	2, 52	8	16	36N.	8 add
Capricorn	3	20	7	5	3, 24	13	14	40S.	11 ſub
Fomalhaut	1	22	44	51	3, 34	30	48	31S.	19 add
Pegaſus	1	22	53	32	3, 0	13	58	27N.	19 add
Andromeda		23	56	44	3, 4	27	50	53N.	20 add

The Reader is deſired to correct the following errors,

Page 7, line 5 from the bottom, for Col. ½ Elap. T. read Coſ. of Riſing.
Page 9, line 3, for P. M. read A. M. any other errors may be corrected at Sight.

N. B. As a new Edition of the PRACTICAL NAVIGATOR and SEAMAN's NEW DAILY ASSISTANT is going to Preſs, with great Improvements, Remarks from any Gentleman who can contribute towards the correcting the Latitude and Longitude of Places, Time of High Water, &c. will be thankfully received by Meſſ. RICHARDSON and URQUHART, under the Royal-Exchange, London.

F I N I S.

www.ingramcontent.com/pod-product-compliance
Lightning Source LLC
Chambersburg PA
CBHW021230260626
47172CB00002B/695
* 9 7 8 3 7 4 1 1 2 7 5 6 4 *